Following an order from the official, he tugs down one and then the other shoulder of his singlet. The wrestling outfit falls to his waist.

The crowd roars. Roger is obviously humiliated. He's not used to this role in the game.

The rest of the singlet comes down and he's standing in only his supporter; his firm, hairy buttocks are now exposed to our view. Then, he pulls off even the supporter. Again, the official commands him to display himself. Naked, his cock beginning to rise in the fear or anticipation of what will happen, Roger is forced to walk the perimeter of the entire ring.

When the official is satisfied that we have seen what we deserve to, he brings Roger back to the center of the ring. Now Roger kneels. Those of us who adore the details of the matches watch the little movements, those things we admire and treasure: We see that Roger has clenched his fists in anger and defeat, they move behind his back now, but don't relax. We focus in on his nipples, watching them rise up erect through the coating of his body hair and displaying their pink skin for us. His stomach is heaving, the cuts of his abdominal muscles are clearly visible.

Now, and only now, does the official wave in an anxious James. The blond youngster jumps across the stage and stands in front of his former adversary. He strips quickly and completely, not waiting for any orders ... The official nods his head and it's time to proceed.

cover art by F. Ronald Fowler

ENTERTAINMENT FOR A
MASTER

John Preston

Alyson Publications, Inc. · Boston

Also by John Preston

Classified Affairs
(with Frederick Brandt)

Deadly Lies

Franny: The Queen of Provincetown

Golden Years

I Once Had a Master

Stolen Moments

Sweet Dreams

Copyright © 1986 by John Preston. All rights reserved.
Cover art copyright © 1986 by F. Ronald Fowler.

This is a paperback original from Alyson Publications, Inc.,
PO Box 2783, Boston, MA 02208.

Distributed in England by GMP Publishers,
PO Box 247, London, N15 6RW.

First U.S. edition, May 1986
ISBN 0 932870 94 5

The Ad
7

The Reaction
9

The Thought
13

The First Interview
31

The Replies
38

Teaching
56

The Place
71

A Duet
78

Preparations
100

The Beginning
107

Martin
114

A Military Presence
118

Questions
124

An Interruption
130

The Morning
139

The End
156

To V.K. McCarty

The Ad

Volunteers Needed

For a very private, very elegant S&M party for a discreet group of ladies and gentlemen to be held in San Francisco. Men must be well built and attractive, willing and able to perform servile tasks and endure moderate to heavy pain. Only the very willing and the experienced need apply.

The Reaction

The phone calls began the moment the advertisement appeared. Of course it hadn't mentioned my name or telephone; these were people who recognized the box number in the return address. These were not the new and unexplored ones I had hoped to hear from. Instead I was getting the reactions of people who already knew me.

The first, interestingly, was from the editor of a periodical in which the notice appeared. I thought perhaps I was being called to talk about an article. But he quickly brought me around to the real subject at hand. "What are you doing?"

I still hadn't a clue and made some inappropriate response about a project. "No, no," he said excitedly, "What are you doing at that party? Can I come? I want to be there."

I laughed at him. He was one of those terribly cleancut young professionals who always disdain those certain elements of my sexuality they find socially unacceptable — at least they do in public or in print. But when there appeared even a small likelihood that I was holding a function where he could become a participant, then the other part of my life was glamorous — so long, I'm sure, as no one would know of his involvement.

I waved the comments off. "No, no, it's a special event, only a very few people. And what, by the way, were you doing reading those classified ads? I didn't even think you were aware they existed."

That shut him up. The responsible image he tries to project isn't compatible with looking in prurient classifieds, even if they do pay his salary. He was seldom caught admitting that he did.

His call wasn't an isolated incident. Many people I knew had discovered the notice and decided that this event had sufficient potential that they would broach with me the subject of attending. Other authors, none who would dare write erotic literature, suddenly found my activities entrancing. The most obnoxious thought they could cover their reactions by joking about my party.

I wasn't in the mood for that to happen. I simply turned those off completely. To a few others, people I respected, I explained that the event was for Madame and Adrienne, and that Phil would be the only other man. It was set up only for the four of us.

Implicit was the statement that only the four of us would properly enjoy the entertainment that was planned. That was too harsh a judgment, but it had some reality to it. I had certainly hosted other events where many more guests had been in attendance and everything had gone on perfectly, but this party was a special performance.

It was my own re-entrance into the life that I had left behind five years ago. I had moved to the country, bored by the city that had become more of a distraction to my work than a stimulation. In my rural home, the opportunities for the carnival sex life I had left were few and far between. I was more dependent on the visits of strangers and the kindness of friends who were willing to travel the long miles, at least in summer. Winter visitors in the north country are rare beasts indeed.

But now I'd be in San Francisco. Madame, my beloved if difficult friend, would be there at the same time. Phil lives across the Bay in one of those industrial cities. Above all, there'd be Adrienne, the elegant author who had filled all our nights with fantasies.

The world the four of us shared was one of words and photographs and of appeals to higher planes of sexuality. Madame, Phil, and I had all aspired to it for years. We had learned its outline by living it in the sexual ghettoes of the modern urban world. There is still, in some ways, the smell of those places on us. We don't deny that. We nurture the memory of the odors fondly.

But Adrienne has joined us on her own. Her path has been less convoluted, her message more beautiful in a way. If her descriptions are less realistic, they are all the more precious for their eloquence.

Our circle is joined by separate lines. The distances between Madame's townhouse in New York, Adrienne's Victorian mansion in San Francisco, Phil's adored retreat in the East Bay and my own country home span thousands of miles.

We had each met in couples over the years, but never had there been a time when we four could sit in the same room and smoke cigarettes, enjoy conversation, simply be in one another's company.

Madame is ready to ritualize anything we can. It is her desire, her hope that she lend beauty to life with displays of courtly manners and appreciation of grace.

Phil had been so much a part of the sexual world that he could judge what were the most perfect sexual events. He could sit and watch any scenario I could develop and enjoy every element that I had worked to add to the piece. It follows, of course, that he could be my most severe critic. If my idea lacked authenticity, it was he who would pounce on me and actually be offended.

Adrienne would have her chance to see it all happening. She had been anxious in our conversations to know the details, to discover just how movements were made. Her fantasy life had been rich, but her actual experiences had been limited. For her own reasons, she wouldn't want to participate in the few opportunities that other people could offer her.

I could do that. I could make this event happen for her. I could offer Madame a chance to see service in perfection. I could make this party an offering to Phil, a thank you for the years of education he'd given me.

At a book convention? Where else? Why not? It was our chance to be together.

Other callers claimed I was doing this only for the sake of shocking the establishment around me. That wasn't my intention. But someone passed on the ad to the organization sponsoring the convention. Somehow the message had been garbled and they were convinced that I planned a demonstration on the floor of the convention. I found the idea humorous, and couldn't keep from laughing, and wasn't able to hide the fact that publicity was the furthest thing from my mind.

My mind was on re-entering the sexual world — with a vengeance. Why? That's one of the questions I've learned not to ask.

My fantasies dictated it. My urges demanded it. My desires warranted it. It had been a long time since I had explored these things in reality. I had made my retirement from the scene for a period of time and I intended to return to the country again. But now I wanted to make this one step.

I had lived my life, before leaving the cities, by merging fantasy with reality. I had gone out and done things that other people would whisper about. I had not been harmed, and harming others didn't interest me. I was interested in the beauty of sex and the possibilities of dreams coming true.

My current vision was accessible. I could achieve it with integrity. I could make a gift of an extraordinary evening to three important people in my life. I saw no reason not to attempt it.

One of my callers complained that to imbue my sexual activities with so much glamour was dangerous, it would make them more desirable to people who shouldn't be enticed into my particular sexual practices. I immediately rejected that argument. My sexual thoughts and actions are many things, but they are not hypocritical and they are not produced to do anything but give immense pleasure.

Who do I think I am? the caller asked me. What right do I have to take the private acts of sexuality and the fantasies of people and make them events, write about them, photograph them, lead them into being real?

I am the ringmaster of the circus. I direct the lights and I coordinate the acts. That is my skill, my first love, my contribution to a world full of blandness and dreary morality.

I knew from the start that my party would be a success.

The Thought

The idea of sexual service produces horror and strange anger in our society. It's sad. People find no problem with forcing teenagers to work in disgusting fast food shops, or with women being sent to the most meaningless tasks in department stores, or about the kinds of jobs minority men are assigned to. But when the option of sexual labor is presented, there's an outcry.

The vehemence of the protest has little to do with reality. At least some prostitutes of both sexes continue to stand up and say they enjoy their work and receive adequate compensation, but they're never believed. Stars of pornographic movies can relate their intense personal enjoyment in the indulgence of their sexual exhibitionism, but the overseers of our morals demand that these people must be unhappy.

Even more stupid is the denial that we, as a culture, already drench ourselves in a sort of sexual slavery. So long as the words are never used we don't have to acknowledge the ways we honor and utilize sexual service. We deride pornography but grace the pages of our finest magazines with suggestive photographs of handsome men and women in their underwear. We send out young college men onto football fields where we demand they earn their educations by exhibiting intense physical sadomasochism for our enjoyment.

That example, college football, is one of the most amazing for me. I am a passionate fan of the sport, tending to follow those teams where the athletic directors seem to be at least unconsciously aware of their purpose and so dress the players in uniforms that are cut to reveal strong stomachs. While I sit and study the gridiron stars with my cock hard and my fantasies running rampant, I identify with my predecessors in ancient Rome.

These are our gladiators. These young men have turned themselves over to sadistic coaches who force them through appalling physical exercises. They've entered into a period of bound servitude much like that used in colonial America where free Europeans would sign over a period of their lives to a master in return for a future reward — citizenship, or perhaps land to settle upon that would be otherwise too expensive. In the same way these athletes give up their youth in hope of an education or some other prize.

For that future compensation these men will perform on the field, vying for my attention, experiencing untold tortures for my enjoyment, displaying their bodies in often obscene juxtaposition with other men's for my titillation. But, we're told, this is not sex. This is simple amateur sport. The farce becomes obvious when the season ends and the tallies of the universities' profits are made public.

I would much rather that the sexual reality of our lives and the desire of some of us for sexual service were open and honest. If I am to receive sexual pleasure from young men in return for my payment and my loyal following of their careers, then the world of sport could deliver that to me with much greater efficiency than it does now if only they would wipe away the moral hypocrisy that has infused our thinking.

What would my fantasy be?

Of course, there would be many options, but let me follow through with the example of athletics. We pay exorbitant amounts of money to enjoy the images of professional wrestlers making fools of themselves in staged and comic sport. We rob those men of their stature. I would rather see a situation where they're not deprived of their elegance. My view, of course, demands the acceptance by all of us that there is dignity in work. A job well done and amply rewarded should be respected.

Here is the way I wish professional wrestling were set up:

There would be a public space, an amphitheater, where the ring would be surrounded by a limited number of seats. The cost would be high, but the entertainment value so immense that many of us would pay the admission. We would be seated in the round and wait for the wrestlers to arrive.

They would be handsome young men, well trained and fed, given the best exercise programs and the most comfortable living arrangements to compensate for their hard labor. When two of them entered the ring, a hush would come over the crowd. There might be an occasional remark, a little joke, a pointed comment on the perfection of the bodies we were viewing, but nothing more.

The men would wear protective headgear and athletic supporters and boots. They would have on the wrestling singlets that are so highly sexual.

The rules would be strictly enforced by a referee. There would be no set-up here; the winner and loser have too much to lose or gain to even think of throwing the fight.

Imagine that there are two men now. Let's give them names and personal features. There's James. He's the younger, only twenty. He's smooth-skinned, blond, his hair is close-cropped and his eyes sparkle. They're that shade of blue that seems to lose its color in bright sunlight. He's anxious for the match to begin. He's waited for this moment when he could enter the ring for this big challenge of his.

His opponent is Roger. He's only slightly older, twenty-five, but he's a veteran of the ring by now. He's calmer, less enthused in a way. But he's hardly taking the event lightly. Another win will move him further forward in his life choices. Besides, while James is focused on the match, Roger is already interested in the outcome.

Roger is dark-haired. His head is covered with short, tight curls and his chest has a full mat. His legs, too, are hirsute and his arms as well. But there isn't such a covering that the firm, finely etched muscles aren't obvious to every one of us looking at him.

The match begins. The two men start in a traditional greco-roman position. They struggle as James finds an unexpected reservoir of strength and — almost too quickly — Roger is pinned. The younger blond man hears the official's announcement and jumps up, throwing his hands over his head in a victory stance. "Not so quick, youngster," someone from the audience jeers at him. "Don't think that fine butt of yours is safe yet!"

The expression on Roger's face has darkened. He hadn't

thought the younger one could do it. But the veteran's polish is coming through now. There is a determination that underlines the impact of the other cries coming from the crowd. "What, Roger, are you so horny you're going to throw the fight?"

No. Not at all. The two men resume their positions. The official signals them to start. Just as quickly as his opponent had moved before, Roger now finds the right moves and acts at just the right times and James finds himself flattened and helpless on the ring floor.

It's a tie. When the two men stand this time and face one another, the crowd goes wild. "Who gets it?" one woman screams from a far corner. "Save some for me, Roger," a man yells across the way.

The combatants are oblivious to the sounds now. Their moments of truth are coming closer. Again, the official calls them to their positions. Again, they take their stance. The signal is made and they begin their final attempt.

The sweat has plastered Roger's body hair to his skin. The strain on his face shows his determination. There's just as much of the sweat and resolution on James. This match lasts much longer, so long that James's youth shows. Tears flow from his eyes from the pain and the agony of the confrontation. Perhaps, too, he's in touch with his fear of what might follow if he loses. Maybe the full force of that hadn't struck him until now. After all, it's his first big match and no matter how many private showings and practice sessions there might have been, nothing can prepare a wrestler for the crowd and its noises and its rough verbal demands.

They sneak and slip out of one another's embraces. There seems to be no end. The first two times were so quick, but now the audience is getting its money's worth as the gladiators vie for the win. It looks, for an exciting moment, as though Roger has done it, conquered the young upstart. But there's a quick movement, a lucky hold, and the audience cheers with delight as the older man is pinned, his shoulders immobile and his defeat obvious to everyone even before it's declared by the official.

Now comes the climatic scene, the reason for the crowd's delight. Waiters and waitresses rush through the stands to deliver beverages, knowing the guests will want refreshment.

Not that there's any break in the action on the stage. The official has, appropriately, moved right on to the next part of the performance. He stands in his uniform and puts his fists on his waist. James has been sent to his corner, but Roger remains in the center of the ring.

He lowers his eyes, refusing to answer the catcalls and whistles that have increased in their intensity. He unties his high boots while kneeling on the stage. He stands when the shoes and socks have been removed and, following another order from the official, he pulls off first one and then the other shoulder of his singlet. The wrestling outfit falls to his waist.

The crowd roars. Roger is obviously humiliated. We don't care if it's by this or by the idea of having lost a match for the first time in months. He's not used to this role in the game and it only increases our pleasure in viewing him.

The rest of the singlet comes down and he's standing in only his supporter, his firm, hairy buttocks are now exposed to our view. Those of us who've not seen them before are able to get a good look at them as he is forced to slowly revolve on the stage.

Then, he pulls off even the supporter. Again, the official commands him to display himself. Now, naked and his cock beginning to rise in the fear or anticipation of what will happen, Roger is forced to walk the perimeter of the entire ring. His pace must be slow, when he goes too fast the official correctly reprimands him and forces him to move backwards to any place where the audience might have been cheated of a good opportunity to investigate his attractiveness.

Until this moment the match has been a totally legitimate sport. But now the game is the enjoyment of the crowd. They are here to view and it's the official's job to make sure their pleasure is delivered. He doesn't mind that Roger is sulking as he goes through his humiliation. He knows that many of us enjoy that, we think of it as an additional element of authenticity that the young man should be having so much trouble fulfilling his obligations — at least we do so long as the obligations are, in fact, fulfilled.

Only when the official is satisfied that we have seen what we deserve to does he bring Roger back to the center of the ring. Now Roger kneels. Those of us who adore the details of the matches watch the little movements, those things we admire and treasure: We see that Roger has clenched his fists in anger and defeat, they move behind his back now, but don't relax. We focus in on his nipples, watching them rise up erect through the coating of his body hair and displaying their pink skin for us. His stomach is heaving, the cuts of his abdominal muscles are clearly visible.

Everyone, of course, watches his cock. The wrestlers have been trained in sexuality. They may loath defeat and its consequences, but a veteran like Roger would have found the pleasures as well. It's swelling. The official reaches over and pats Roger on the head. The defeated wrestler has executed his role well. His cock is getting hard and rising up in an arc whose angle increases. He also holds his body stiff. His head is lowered, he's still not going to look into the eyes of the crowd. But he'll follow through and give a good show.

Now, and only now, does the official wave in an anxious James. The blond youngster jumps across the stage and stands in front of his former adversary. He strips quickly and completely, not waiting for any orders and not lingering at any stage. He is not obligated to put on that show. Not now, at least.

Naked, his long pale cock is already hard and the men and women in the audience make lewd jokes about the sexual abilities of youngsters. He plays with them, stroking himself and pointing his erection at one man in particular, obviously hoping he might earn some special favors from that audience member later in the day. He cups his balls and holds them up, rubbing the sweat off them. He's the victor, he's earned this right to be lordly, if only for a short time.

The official nods his head and it's time to proceed.

He hands Roger a condom. The man unwraps it and carefully applies it to his victor's cock. The latex stretches glistening over the tight skin. Then, Roger follows tradition and leans forward. He purses his lips and kisses the head of his conqueror's cock. It must be done slowly and softly and reverently. He must display a meaningful admission of his role now.

The official accepts his action. James says something we can't hear. The official barks the command that Roger should obey. His mouth opens and he leans forward, his clenched fists still behind his back. He takes in the entire length of the younger man's erection. The official makes another order, he's apparently unsatisfied. Closer, he must have seen some evidence that Roger was not doing well enough because now we see Roger's chest expanding and tighten. He's obviously choking. He must not have taken all of the young man in him before.

It is all up to James now. The audience shouts out suggestions to him. He laughs when someone says he should change position with Roger. He has no intention of doing that. Instead he crosses his arms over his chest. He moves his thighs, letting his hips guide his cock in and out of Roger's mouth. The inward thrusts cause the defeated gladiator great discomfort. Each one seems to produce a seizure of choking. That angers the crowd. They want more grace in these actions, much more.

If James wanted to, he could prolong Roger's anguish and probable later punishment. But no, that's not his desire. He is fixated on something else, just as a youngster would be. He withdraws his cock, then gives an order and Roger immediately complies, knowing he has no choice and expecting this very thing in any event.

He swivels, still on his knees, until his back is to the younger man. Then he leans forward until his forehead touches the ground. His ass is left high in the air. James now kneels down as well. He playfully slaps one of the cheeks of Roger's ass and draws an appreciative round of applause from the audience.

The covered cock moves in to the dark cleft of Roger's buttocks, separating the hair. We all know that, as part of their preparation, both men were well lubricated before the match. In fact, it would have been possible for us to watch that happening if we had chosen to pay a small premium. Many people find the image of the two wrestlers bending over and being probed by expert greased hands the most delightful of all the events around the wrestling match.

In any case, James has no trouble entering Roger. He moves in with one long stroke that brings a rush of blood to Roger's face. Now the young blond man's body begins to thrust much more strongly than it did while his pleasure had been simply from Roger's mouth.

We can watch the buttocks clench and release with every entry and removal. "Show it, let us see it," screams a man across the way. James smiles. It will only add to Roger's experience of humiliation to have that happen, so the young man does just what is requested, each thrust removing his cock entirely from his victim's body and forcing Roger to experience the entry totally every time.

There's only so long this can continue. The official speaks to James, he should finish. The crowd wants the action to be complete, but they wanted it to be part of a quick moving plot. There are more characters waiting in the wings for more struggles.

James picks up his speed and soon there's a vitality to his fucking that undeniably announces his approaching orgasm. Then, a loud roar builds up from his belly into his chest and the crowd begins to respond with even greater enthusiasm. James's belly contracts tightly, the red blush of his orgasm spreads up and out from the center and his eyes clamp shut. He collapses on top of Roger, his chest sweat merging with the rivulets that run down the other man's back.

The crowd erupts into applause. It's been a good fight, a finer ending. James pulls out his cock and — as tradition decrees — unravels the condom. The latex is upended and the white ooze of his seminal fluid pours onto the stage. Another round of applause, not only for him, but also in appreciation for the raging erection that Roger has no ability to hide.

His cock is sweeping away from his body, almost pointing straight into the air. Sometimes a wrestler will orgasm from being fucked in the ring. The audience always considers that a cheat. They want to see submission and they might appreciate a display of perfect training in another context, but here in the ring — no — they want to see struggle and defiance. Roger's cock gives them that proof.

He's not allowed to touch it, of course, and so must let it painfully swing ahead of him while he follows James out of the ring. Those of us who come here often make a mental note to watch future wrestling notices. There will, inevitably, be a rematch and we will certainly want to be here for it.

Now, we have a choice. The wrestling will continue and another pair of gladiators is waiting. But, instead, let me take you through the rest of the compound that exists in my imagination. It is a rich place, full of particulars and I want you to see as many of them as we can.

You see, this is not just a question of a wrestling match. The matches are only a part of the activities, the most public and the ones that most people will come to. There are many people who aren't interested in finer elements of the compound or else they have other means of reaching their sexual pleasures and don't use this exact outlet.

The men who are wrestlers are all here for a period of time. How long? Perhaps five years; some longer. How did they get here? Perhaps some have simply decided this is the way to earn their way through the same college education that our football players expect as their own payment. Others might have been petty criminals, young men who committed nonviolent crimes and who a judge decided needed the discipline that the wrestling camp can provide. Or they might be young men who wanted to have a larger nest egg to start their careers with than the mistakes of birth had given them. There are certainly those who simply wanted to be wrestlers. The society where these events are taking place, remember, doesn't degrade the men who have these experiences, in fact, we all think they develop character. There have been many young men who have listened to the appreciative comments of the crowds and the stories that are told and who have always aspired to join this troupe.

The men train constantly and their workouts are outdoors. We can walk behind the stadium and find dozens of them developing their physiques with weights. They have on only the slightest garment, to give just enough support for their genitals that they don't harm themselves.

Otherwise, they are naked as they work with weights and various physique machines. The crowd cannot interfere with their concentration — some of these devices could be dangerous — but we are welcome to walk through their yard and come as close as we wish to them. We can study up close just how they are developing. Many onlookers have adopted favorites and make a sport of coming to watch each one of the them as their chests are expanded, or their buttocks tightened, or whatever.

There are some who adore the sight of the strain the men go through. While today's athletic directors might use threats or intimidations to force young men to work harder, this camp exists in a fantasy of sexual service. Here, instead, there are men and some women who stand by and watch as their favorite goes through a particularly grueling set of exercises and finally appears to give up in fatigue. Then the patron or patroness makes an offer: Do another set of the workout and there'll be a special payment.

The young men will always do what they can to comply, going back to the machines or the weights and struggling with all their might and will to do whatever is necessary to earn the tip that's been offered. Some men have made astonishing progress with their physical development because of this little added touch.

Notice over there, the red-headed woman who's standing by one of the wrestlers doing gymnastics. He's just finished an appalling number of sit-ups. His stomach is so tight that we can trace all of his abdominal muscles. She's not satisfied, evidently. She leans over and whispers in his ear. The reward she's offering must be quite large. He sighs, almost in dread, but resumes his position and begins to do the exercises again. He strains, his stomach is rebelling against the torture she's demanded. But he continues while she counts each one of the sit-ups. They must have been enough. She smiles, tousles his hair and calls over the official to have the young man's reward entered into his book. If he's really attracted her affection in his workouts, the athlete will soon amass a large amount in his savings for his future.

Walk this way, past the place where the athletes shower. They, of course, have no privacy. They've given that up for the salaries they've contracted to earn. Some people even go to watch them sleep, finding the young male bodies in repose the most beautiful of their masculine positions. Others simply adore watching the common activities of daily life as they're carried out by nude men, as though the voyeurism can be more intense by being made ordinary.

But this is my favorite of those quiet moments of spying — the watching of the athletes while they shower. Stand here and look at them. Each has his own style, that one embarrassed because you see him soaping up the crevice of his buttocks and that other one exhibiting himself shamelessly, knowing full well that you're studying him while he lathers his genitals.

My friend Laurence talks of having lived in Berlin one summer. There is, he says, a nude gay beach in that city. He used to promenade there, fully clothed, holding his walking stick while he wandered around the littered naked bodies. The feeling he experienced he termed, "Olympian." That is just how I sense this sensation, this standing here watching a line of naked men, all of them aware — painfully or joyfully — that they are being observed by clothed and appreciative onlookers. This is a special joy, to be able to be so blatant about the pleasure and not have to play silly games about happening upon someone or else trying to catch random, unnoticeable views.

They should have a series of tables here. I've mentioned it to the officials. I, for one, would gladly spend an afternoon occasionally, sipping wine and watching the men as they move from the exercise area to the other, more... interesting arenas.

When the athletes need a break from their workout, they go to the food tent. They are, of course, well fed and would never be allowed to actually go hungry or experience anything else that would truly harm them. But in this part of the compound the food and drink is only available to the customers. To be served, the young men must beg from a patron.

Besides, the young men are forbidden to have any cash. That's the purpose of the official carrying around the book. To allow the wrestlers to have money would give them the freedom to circumvent the customers too often; it would leave them with a false sense of their time here in the compound.

Don't worry, their compensation is carefully and honestly recorded. Their payments at the end of their service are often huge. They often return as customers. It's said the other wrestlers fear them most; they're the most demanding of all. There is no cheating going on here. But the idea of the penniless athlete who must come to the visitor and ask for even the smallest piece of fruit or something as simple as a glass of water is one of the appeals of the compound.

Cajoling words are seldom a pleasant enough attraction, though occasionally someone will reward a wrestler who's earned them good money from a bet. But more often a small service must be exchanged. Nothing too demanding. What then? Imagine that tall and slender brown-skinned wrestler you admire so much. He's entered the tent wearing only his supporting garment. He approaches you and smiles — he knows the games that go on here. He asks if you wouldn't please give him a glass of juice.

Not while he's wearing that piece of clothing, you say. He

smirks, expecting this, and removes it. His long, thin cock swings free, you tell him how much you'd like to touch it. Make him move forward and stand on his toes to lift his cock and balls up until he can lay them on the palm of your outstretched hand.

Perhaps you'd rather he turned around and showed you how perfectly his buttocks are developing. Make him wiggle them for you, or else, bend over and separate them if you'd rather study how nicely his anus is placed.

The wrestlers can never join the customers at their tables, but are expected to stay close while they enjoy whatever's been bought for them. Your young man is given his juice by a waitress. He kneels appreciatively by your side, letting you catch the delicious aroma of his honestly earned sweat while you play with his hair and test the flesh of his shoulders. He will occasionally look up at you while you sip your own wine and answer your questions about the wrestling camp. He'll tell you how much he enjoys it.

Now is the time the young men show how much they understand the dynamics here. The naked youth tries to talk to you about the rest of your activities. He'll time his presence on the block if he thinks you're interested enough to offer a good enough price. Maybe, just to entice you more, he'll lean forward and rest his head against your crotch, rubbing gently to make your cock harden with passion.

Perhaps he pleases you enough with his conversation that you decide to reward him with a piece of fruit. No, don't just give it to him, have him eat it out of your palm. He'll do it carefully and thankfully, making sure to clean up your hand with his tongue.

This is all within the expected. Our fantasy society doesn't think in violent and extreme terms always. The natural grace and elegance of service is often a quiet pleasure and there's really nothing quite so lovely as a well developed, nude body in repose.

But after the refreshment, there's more. Much more.

The wrestling compound is highly disciplined. It must be. Controlling the activities and the energies of so many young men is difficult without a firm hand. Some of the patrons would, of course, love to be the ones who determined the extent of the punishment, but there'd be little chance the athletes would have the strength or energy to fulfill their other duties if they had to constantly act out the lusts of those customers. There's another way to accomplish the necessary goals.

The paid officials of the camp have a strict and highly structured list of punishments for each of a number of transgressions. Some call for extreme forms of humiliation, especially if the officials determine that the cause of the violation is a too-strong ego. Around the punishment area are naked, bound men, stretched out with their bodies curved over padded workhorses in a way that their asses are pulled apart and their cocks and balls left hanging. Little leather-covered paddles are near by. Patrons are able to pick them up and deliver blows while a careful official watches.

The cries of the men seem to fill the place with so much sound that one can barely hear the whack of the paddles against the tender flesh. But these are almost more painful mentally than physically. More serious crimes offer patrons more serious pleasures. Some men have been stood up against posts, their hands tied above their heads and their feet firmly secured to the bottom of the pole. Beside them are signs, each one detailing the punishment assigned to the athlete. For a set sum, the patron can buy the honor of delivering these chastisements if he chooses to pay the price.

The more knowledgeable wrestlers strain their necks and struggle to see who it is that is putting the coins in the official's hands. There are loud moans if the patron is recognized as one who knows how to use the long thin length of leather that will be handed to him.

There's Hugo, the wonderfully developed bodybuilder you've admired before. The price the official is demanding to deliver the five blows that have been decreed for Hugo isn't that much. Pay it. Enjoy giving the arrogant athlete his punishment.

The bound wrestler is yours to touch and feel in any way you choose. Go ahead, give him some preliminary slaps of the buttocks with your hand. Make his ass flesh jump, feel that strength. Now explore him sexually the way you've always wanted to. Don't be gentle. The man is being punished, after all. Grab his balls harshly and pull until you can hear that his pain is honest and that his pleas for relief are heartfelt. Pull the sac back and stretch it out until the testicles are pressed firmly against the skin.

Now he knows you're serious. Pinch his nipples hard, first one then the other. Watch how much he struggles to free himself even though he knows it's impossible. Aren't his enormous muscles gorgeous in this bondage? Don't his struggles make them seem even more beautiful and more desirable than ever before?

Now stand back. Remember, you're being carefully watched by the official. Take the long leather strap he holds out for you and swing it in the air to get the feel for it. Also, you want to let Hugo know you're going to use it with great competence. Now deliver the punishment with firm, carefully counted blows. The flesh of the buttocks rises in color, the pale curves of white skin take on sudden lines of red and flushes of pink with each application of the leather.

When it's over, Hugo is let down. But his punishment is not over. You have also bought the next step. Hugo, still sobbing from his ordeal, comes over to you and kneels in front of you. He reaches up and your pants are carefully opened by the chastised wrestler. He reaches in and brings out your cock. He covers it with the omnipresent latex and then kisses its tip. Through the layer of reflecting protection, the young man sucks and licks, his tongue moving to try to nurture you. The faster he can achieve the patron's pleasure, the sooner he'll be released. And there's always the worry that you could claim dissatisfaction. That's to be avoided at all costs since it could lead to still further punishments.

I'll move away while you take your pleasure from Hugo's willing tongue and lips. Let me know when you're ready to move on...

There? Wasn't he worth waiting for and didn't the knowledge that you'd given him such a fine thrashing make it all the better?

In the next compound there's another crowd. Let's move over to it. It's even more obviously sexually excited than any other group has been before. The people stand around a raised platform, a small one, with room just enough for a single man to stand comfortably. This is the place where the wrestlers earn their real money.

At any time an athlete can stand in line to walk up the stage. It is a choice always open to him. Perhaps he found a man back at the restaurant who wanted much more than a slight kiss or an erotic exposure. Then they could agree to move here. Of course, they both run the risk that the patron will be outbid by others. But that seldom happens.

It's more common that a young man has completed the daily

round of exercises and wants to relieve his own pressures and continue to build up his savings. He gets in line and waits, looking out at the crowd and wondering who will buy his services.

You're concerned about the idea of the wrestlers selling themselves? Clear your mind. Realize this: No man walks up onto that stage unless he wants to. He chooses the time. It's his desire to earn the money. Yes, of course, once the sale is complete he loses control over the events. But if he wants to retain control, he only has to decide not to mount the stage.

Why is the idea of the sale so bothersome? The man has things about him that others desire. He'll not be irrevocably harmed by having them used; he'll receive just compensation; he understands what it is about and is informed. Love doesn't come from a slave auction, of course not. But just who is it that decreed love is a part of sexual pleasure?

Purchasing the services of a decent housekeeper or a fine secretary isn't frowned upon, why should you wonder about the gathering of a man's sexual abilities?

As each man is called up, an official stands beside him, right by the stage. His role is passive. He is only there to hear and record the financial transactions. It's up to the athlete to produce the bids. He must present himself at his best, offering with his body and his words the most pleasure possible in order to elicit the greatest offers.

Imagine that it's James on the platform, flush and cocky from his victory in the ring. He would know that some of the audience would rush here hoping he'd be smart enough to offer his victorious and well displayed body. He's standing there, naked. His cock is softer now, but he's healthy and young, and he and the rest of us are confident he'll still be able to perform well for us.

He's smiling at the crowd. He runs a hand over his upper body, pinching each of his pink nipples. He licks his fingers and wets the two little pinpoints on his chest, making sure the liquid highlights the color.

Now he reaches down and cups his testicles, lifting them up to us. They're light-colored with the same blond hair on them as the rest of his body. They are young, held tightly to his torso. Over them is his cock. He reaches for it now, stroking it lovingly and coaxing it in hopes of an erection.

But these aren't the things that often interest the patrons and James knows that. He turns around and displays his ass. It's quite beautiful, hairless, round, standing up in smooth arches. He spreads his legs and then reaches both hands back to pull apart his buttocks. Roger had done this at the ring, but he'd been forced to, it had been sexually exciting, but not erotic in the same way. This young man now is displaying himself in hopes that you'll buy him for an hour's entertainment.

After all, the athletes have been as well trained in producing our erotic pleasures as they have in their other work. Those mouths and hands and asses all have been coached by the best in the land to deliver ultimate enjoyment.

The image of James's small and naked hole sends a shiver through the crowd. He's achieved his hope. He'll get the highest bids today. When the figures are shouted through the air, he turns and smiles down on the crowd with obvious delight. He encourages each and every bidder to go higher. One man wants to know what he'd look like on his knees with his mouth open to receive a hard cock. Immediately, James takes the position. Another wants to know what James would have looked like if he had been the vanquished in the ring. It's not an insult. The young man spins around on the platform where he barely has room to lift up his ass and display himself.

Each of the actions is mischievously committed, always with a smile. There's a purpose to coming to the stand and offering oneself to the auction, and a bad attitude has no place here. Finally the sale is over, and the official makes a note in James's book to record his earnings.

James jumps down and walks to the winner. When he gets there the man grabs hold of his hair and yanks it. The smile goes from James's face. He falls to the ground and leans forward to find a hard cock waiting behind the patron's pants. Once the bidding is over, there is no limit to the ownership. The man pulls a short leash and collar from his pocket and wraps it around James's neck. They leave, the athlete who was so recently the victorious conqueror now scurrying on hands and knees to be taken to a private room where he will have no release until the patron is satisfied his money was well spent.

But if this is the way it ends for the victor, what happened to the one he defeated? There's still another compound and the cries and groans become louder as you approach it.

Here is the place a patron really finds the value of his money. All the losers are in service here for a day after their defeat. The rules don't allow for any great physical punishment in this area, but every one of the wrestlers here has a decidedly pink set of buttocks. Spanking with a hand is only their due in the place where the vanquished spend their time.

But that is the least of their concerns. All the young men are naked. They are running around the space trying to fill the commands that the rules say any patron can give. They have mouths that have been working on hard cocks for seemingly endless hours. Their anuses have been fucked often. At a quick snap of a finger, each one must bend over and receive a patron's cock.

That, though, isn't the worst. There, in the corner, is our Roger. He's being tied to a bench. It allows his feet to reach the ground, but in a way that spreads his muscled, well-haired legs. His hands are also tied tightly to the stand. His stomach and chest and, more important, his abdomen are all parallel now. The patron has reached down and is playing with Roger's cock, rubbing it into a new erection.

The patron is undressed. Once Roger is erect, he applies the latex condom and then straddles himself over Roger, impaling himself on the athlete's cock. Roger moans, actually in agony. This is already the third time he's had to perform since he was led out of the ring and already there's another man and a woman standing around him, playing with his nipples and assuring him that they, too, expect to get service from him.

For his whole time here, Roger's cock will be in agony, constantly forced to an undesired erection and fed into the mouths and anuses and vaginas of anyone who was able to pay the price of admission. If he can't get himself erect? He and all the others assigned this task are forced to work to make sure each and every one of them is taken to the utter limit of his abilities. While the patrons look on, they'll suck and lick one another. They'll be forced into exhibitions if that will please a patron. Their nipples will be weighted with little metal clamps and their testicles will be tied tightly with rawhide. Smoothly shaped dildoes will be implanted in their asses and held in place by ropes. They'll get no rest from it.

Everything possible will be done to arouse them.

The silly people in our society focus on those few tears, a minor number of welts from the necessary punishments and the pink remains of a few spankings. They won't listen to the realities. The tears and the welts and the blush of the buttocks could always be avoided by following the rules and trying harder in the ring. Some punishments in the world are deserved. The experience of them make better men, more understanding of their roles and more willing to learn to carry them out better.

Of course, there are always those men who choose to receive the punishments. There are those wrestlers who find the occasional way to slip in their training and force the officials to send them to the punishment posts. Most athletes would rather place themselves on the selling block to receive money for their futures, but the patrons are often heard to gripe that a few young men sometimes lose a match on purpose, just to find themselves in the area where their cocks and mouths and asses will be put to constant use.

The wrestling camp isn't perfect yet. Even the fantasy has its flaws. But that's part of its humanity, after all. The moralists forget they defy the gods — whatever gods they choose — when they attempt to be godlike in their perfection and forget to indulge in the vagaries of human existence. My wrestlers are not perfect, nor are my patrons. But they are aware that services well rendered and well received produce a tremendous amount of mutual respect.

I can't recreate my wrestling camp. Unfortunately, too many of the moralists have made too many of the potential participants uneasy with their needs and desires. But my party would give me a chance to come close, to see that the men who would answer my advertisement and my guests understood that the services being exchanged were highly valued and the people tremendously respected.

The First Interview

My plan of action was very simple. I had placed the ads and I would soon be receiving answers. I would sift through the replies and decide which people to actually interview. I would be in San Francisco for a full week before the party; that would give me more than enough time to talk to the possible volunteers.

I continued to field the phone calls. I was honestly surprised by some of the people who tracked me down — these were all still people who had a means of knowing who had actually placed the classified and who could get hold of my phone numbers. There was a reporter for a newspaper who wanted to cover the event. There was another magazine editor who wanted to send a photographer to record it. These last ideas were unacceptable. The party was for the four of us and all the attention of the volunteers had to be on us and our pleasure. To have them preening for cameras wouldn't have done at all.

I had not expected the call from Martin.

It was the one I should have hoped for, but I had forgotten how possible it could have been. When I answered and heard his voice I was frozen with a kind of trance. This, truly, was my re-entrance into the old existence I had loved so much and had been away from for so long.

His first sentence — without so much as "Hello" — proved that some things will never end, especially not those that are bonded by the fire and passion of sex. "I saw your ad. I had to call."

"Why not sooner?" I shot out my answer, but there wasn't any anger in it, nor any disappointment, it was just a genuine wonder that we had let it go for so long.

"Things." That was a typical response from him. There would be stories about his life that could entertain me and depress me for hours if I heard them. Martin is one of the pilgrims of the sexual life. There would be many adventures and just as many mishaps over the past few years. I would have to listen to them; they would tell me what had been going on while I had been in retirement.

"How are you?" I asked. "Are you well? Happy? Where are you, for that matter. I can never keep up with you. New York? Key West? Or is it Houston this season?"

"Los Angeles," he replied. "I've been here about a year now."

"Working?"

"On and off. A bartending job for a while. A couple stints as an extra on a big lot. A nice old man who just happened to have an unoccupied cottage on his estate, that kind of thing."

It was the existence Martin had always led. But he could afford to lead it. He was — after all these years — still only about twenty-eight. I had met him when he had lied about his age to enter the sex clubs in New York and the erotic conferences in San Francisco. I had known him when the strange millionaire was transporting him between Europe and North America for single nights of sex.

"I'm delighted to hear from you." It was true. I was and I had a hard cock to prove it. There were memories of Martin that would always make me hard; they are my own private pornography, and their veracity was more potent than anyone else's fiction.

"It's because of your ad."

"That's the reason? Just for that?" I couldn't quite decide if it made me angry or not. A part of me wished he had simply wanted to call me. But then the rest of my mind recalled the other times we'd been together — the times that hadn't been so perfect and had showed another side of him.

"Isn't that enough? It sounds as though you'd want to hear from me if you're doing this. I could help. Besides, I belong there. Aren't I still your boy?"

Of course you are.

His voice was so roguish. He knew precisely what he was doing. He was responding to those small parts of one another that we had each captured. There had been an ad for an event he wanted to take part in. He probably would have done it with anyone, it didn't have to be me. But because it was me, he knew he could move in and take a central role.

He could, I decided. He most certainly could. "I'll need you for the entire weekend."

"I'm working..."

"Take it off. You always can arrange that. You have plenty of notice. I need you."

"We're spending the weekend together?" he asked, a little seduction in his voice.

"You're spending it with me. There'll be a lot of work to be done. Also, I'll be dealing with new volunteers, people I haven't met yet. I'll need to have someone around who can show them the ways things should be done. I've spent a lot of time working on you; if you haven't forgotten your lessons, you'll be a good example for the rest of them."

I spoke as harshly as I could. I didn't want any of this game playing with him. I wanted him. But I remembered now that there were only certain parts of him that I could have. I would simply take all of those elements I was able to and work them for as much as I could — it would be considerable. Very considerable.

He sucked in his breath, I could hear it whistle through his teeth. He knew exactly what I was saying to him. *Of course you're still my boy. I'll make sure you remember that as well as I do.*

"Fine. What are the details? When? Where? How?"

We went through the mechanics and I made him read them back to me from the notes I had made him take. We would meet in San Francisco in a month. It would be a memorable reunion.

* * *

People who are appalled by intense sexuality — the kind that comes clothed in leather and chains and wears whips and handcuffs — usually are so agitated by it that they make many false assumptions. The worst is the idea that there are no emotions involved in it. Their vision of love is one that is filled with roses and gentle sea waves, breezes through pine trees on pristine mountain tops. When the acts they witness are really hurricanes carrying flaming winds, they can only think that they're seeing destruction. They can't perceive the truth — that it is often a more powerful event than anything they have ever imagined.

Martin and I are the proof of that.

Aren't I still your boy?

Forever.

I met him when he was a teenager. I hadn't known that. He was tremendously precocious and was dressed in his authentic navy uniform. The pants were translucent and that first time I had been hypnotized by the outline of his white briefs underneath them. We had been at a party. It was one of those middle class gay affairs mimicking suburbia — a desecration of a desecration.

He was an extraordinarily handsome young man. At least six foot tall, with blond hair and blue eyes, clean shaven with a military haircut and a slightly drawling accent that spoke of a vaguely Southern background.

The men at the party were the type who attempt to make believe that gay men don't have sex at all. They wear suits that are as unsensual as armour and speak about their monogamy and make loud — too loud — judgments on the kind of man who would "betray the cause" by exposing the overtly sexual desires that they, themselves, were denying.

I was a strange person to have among them. But there were many occasions when I would join them for one reason or another. The invitations would come from a work colleague and my agreement to attend would be grounded in a perverse desire to make them all terribly uncomfortable. The presence of a pornographer at one of their soirees was always disconcerting.

Martin's presence was easily explained. One or another of the middle-aged men would always have a presentable youth on hand. One never remarked on the obvious monetary foundation for the relationship, but it was understood. Martin was simply another of a long line. I never did quite understand who he was with. I hardly talked to him, I only studied his midsection and its white cotton bindings. The shape was promising — both front and rear. If his smile hadn't been quite so bright and his stance so easy and comfortable, I might never have let my eyes move above his waist.

I still didn't make my contact with him at the party. But I did find him later that night. I had gone home to change and went to one of the leather bars in vogue in New York that year. I was on the prowl, careful to limit my drinks and never using any other chemical because I was looking for something . . . major. I wanted something that would demand all of my abilities and faculties.

I hadn't expected Martin to come into the same bar, but he did. He was still dressed in his uniform. I thought that was dangerous at first, I had heard him emphasize that he really was a member of the service at the party. But, after a moment I realized that no one in that particular place was going to believe him anyway. It was a social setting predicated on false images and the appearance of reality would go unnoticed.

That was ten years ago. I picked him up easily. But all the details of the night aren't still with me. Instead, I remember discrete moments.

I had a chamber in my apartment set aside for sex. It was well equipped, those were the days when the tools of sex impressed me, or at least interested me. I remember at one point:

Martin is crying, he's hanging down, utterly vulnerable. Wrist and ankle restraints were attached to chains that connected to the ceiling. A belt clamped to another chain supported his midsection. There were pieces of metal attached to his nipples and his scrotum.

Later: I offered to let him go. He was free from the restraints and sitting on the floor, naked. He answered by reaching over on his hands and knees and kissing my foot.

I fucked him. He was flat on his stomach on the floor, I could lift up and see all of his back torso from the buttocks up. His ass cheeks were stripped red with new welts and so, too, were his shoulder blades. I was pounding into him. He was speaking rhythmically, as though chanting a mantra: "Yes, yes, yes, yes. . ."

Afterwards: I was talking to him with the kind of sexual litany that I might use on any man but I suddenly realized this one was listening and this one believed it. "I own you. I will have you again. You will come whenever I tell you to. You are mine."

I remember the morning. The sun had risen and there were small rays that could sneak through the breaks in the curtains that were supposed to block the light from the chamber. Martin was crying. I had reached inside someplace and found something that he didn't want to give up but he realized it was too late. He was sitting on my lap, suddenly a little boy and not the aggressive military male he had presented himself as. He was naked. I had somehow gotten my clothes on. I was rubbing his back. I held him tightly. It was so late; why wasn't I tired? But I don't remember that. I only remember his head on my shoulder and the thought that I never wanted it to be anywhere else, ever.

Even later: We had showered and he was sitting on my lap again. Now he had on those briefs that had entranced me earlier. But that was all. I was once again dressed. This time we were kissing passionately. I reached into his shorts and found his cock hard and oozing from its tip. As though he were somehow someone even younger, I pulled it out, forcing the elastic band of the briefs down to let the whole length of it loose.

I began to pull and tug on the thick, long foreskin that covered it. He only kissed me more, as though that simple act of masturbation were the most intense sexual force he had ever felt. I remember him coming all over my hand, the stuff spilled over and drenched his shorts. I remember us laughing and having to have to shower again.

From that night ten years ago, Martin has been mine. Not always; there were long periods during which we were separated, and only short times together. I don't claim him in those respects; he and I have never been lovers in any traditional sense. But, if I walk into a bar and he's there in whatever city, we never question whether we are going to have sex, only where and how soon. We never question what the roles are; who and what we are to one another is so well established that neither of us ever wants to cross any of the lines we have defined.

Over the years, I have witnessed Martin as much as possessed him, though. We lived in the same sexual world. He had only begun to explore it when we met. It was clear to both of us that he had to make his experiments on his own. I was there as a source of support and a place he could come to talk through the experiences — genital or romantic. But he had to make the journey alone.

It was an exquisite one. He gave himself over to those people who actually train men. He lived once in a dungeon for six months, subjected willingly to every possible sensual torture and used by countless men, many of them masked and personless to him. He lived for a while on a farm that was ruled over by a former military man who insisted that the day-to-day life of the place replicate the most intense boot camp — only with hard-ons and fucking.

He would bring these experiences back to me and offer them

to me, often as a gift. After his training in the dungeon he arrived at my door one night and came in, immediately stripping naked. He smiled as he fell to his knees. He spread his thighs far apart, leaving his testicles vulnerable and exposed. He lifted his head high, throwing out his chest and his prominent nipples. His hands were held behind his back. His hips were placed in a way that his cock was thrust forward. All of those parts of his body that a man might try to protect, Martin offered to me. "Your slave...," was all he said. It was the start of a delicious week.

When he'd gone through the military sex camp he returned in crisply starched and pressed uniform like clothes. Once more he knocked on my door without warning. Again he was smiling. This time he stood at perfect attention and saluted me. "Sir, reporting...," Another week.

I met his boyfriends, sometimes they were men who were putting him through some new sexual encounter, but other times he would make his first attempts to be the leader. I even went on a vacation with him once, to Florida. He had been in a relationship and it hadn't worked. For once, he didn't want me for the sexual frenzy, he needed someone to take care of him in the more gentle ways. When he requested that, I knew that there was no option. Of course I had to agree. That short trip was full of fine meals and good wine, soft talk and only the softest sex. That time was healing. To be chosen to provide the restorative was an honor and I accepted it as such.

Martin would be in San Francisco for my party. I had a month to savor that. I wondered what it would be like to have him in that public setting. He would adore it, and the audience would only intensify his pleasure. And I could be assured that at least one of the volunteers would perform perfectly, absolutely perfectly.

Should I have him serve the food and drink? Or should I recreate that torturous bondage that left him suspended from the ceiling? He would insist on surviving that; no force on earth would make him admit that he couldn't take the test I'd give him.

The last time I had met him he had begun a rigorous bodybuilding program. He had always had a wonderful body, and by now it must be magnificent. I wondered if he shouldn't be simply tied to a piece of furniture so that my guests could enjoy the sight of naked perfection.

The Replies

It didn't take long for the letters to begin arriving. Their democracy astonished me. I had, of course, placed many ads over the years, but it had been a long time and I had forgotten just what a spectrum of types answered them.

There were some scribbled on ruled paper. Others processed on computers. Some were insultingly xeroxed. A few were stupidly challenging. "If you're for real, prove it and perhaps I'll consider your request." This was a response to an advertisement for slaves?

The only ones I considered seriously were those with photographs. A very few others were interesting enough that I did write back to request a picture, but only a couple of those complied.

I built up a folder of the answers. I sorted through them daily, conjuring up wonderful fantasies of just what each of them offered. I wasn't just after a collection of perfect men, I wanted a range of men. I wanted to show Adrienne how diverse the possibilities were and I wanted to impress Madame and Phil with my ability to gather in several distinct types.

I wanted my circus to have many rings.

One by one, the choices made themselves obvious to me and I made the calls. The respondents were all serious, that was my good fortune. I didn't need to deal with the fools who enjoy littering other people's mail with private fantasies that they never expected to be fulfilled.

During the phone calls, I made up my schedule for San Francisco. I had more than enough men from California to be assured of the necessary numbers. I got work schedules from each, told them where to meet me for interviews and how to appear.

Everything went as planned, but there were two replies that were nagging me. Neither one was from California. That made me think that they weren't serious. But there was a sound of intent to them that I couldn't avoid. I decided they deserved attention.

One was from a businessman in Ohio who went so far as to write me on his office stationery, making it a point to declare it a proof of his conviction as well as his ability to afford the trip to the West Coast.

> Dear Sir:
> I've been delirious since I read your ad. My fantasies are decidedly masochistic, but they are also very subtle. The basics of S&M are available in Chicago or New York, cities I visit regularly. I can wear a black leather jacket as well as any other man. My only problem in the bars and parties I go to is that I'm taken for a top more often than not.
>
> I'm 6'4", 32 years old, a conscientious weight lifter with a powerful build as I hope you'll see from the enclosed photographs which are very recent.
>
> But my sexuality isn't satisfied with those activities, especially not today with the health concerns.
>
> I am aware that I am most attracted by the idea of being displayed. I love the attention that I get by exhibiting myself. I'm certain, to be honest, that that's the reason I work out as much as I do.
>
> Your party sounds like an extraordinary possibility for me to realize some of my most secret desires.
>
> I am self employed and can arrange the time off to come to San Francisco for your pleasure. I would be happy to do anything to make your entertainment as complete and perfect as possible.
>
> Forgive me, sir, for admitting this, but my cock is hard and I'm stopping and starting this letter over and over again just to jerk on it enough to keep up the tension that it takes for me to write all of this down.
>
> I've never committed these things to paper before. That's only one indication of how very much your advertisement reached me. But there must be a time when every one of us

says yes to a fantasy.

Being on display in full light, for men and women, with the possibility of being used and abused . . . It's too much, sir. Please accept my humble application.

Your willing slave,
Christopher

The photographs were stunning. This Christopher was even more muscular than I expected Martin to be. The photos showed Christopher in classic bodybuilding poses, wearing one of those very skimpy pairs of briefs that are worn in competition. The artificiality of the posture couldn't hide the smooth bulk he'd built up. He had stopped short of being grotesque, but there was still so much there, so much of him, and the proportions were beautifully displayed.

I was, of course, as interested in the letterhead and his secret desires. This might be one of those men who need to have some balance in their lives. They were often so fascinating, so much in need of a moment of release. I decided I would try this one out. I had the time and the resources for a trip to Ohio on my way West.

I picked up the phone and impulsively dialed his office number. A receptionist answered and passed me on to a secretary. I was officiously told that he was very busy. I insisted that it was very important. With a grudge in her voice, she put me on hold. She came back in a moment and told me that he was unable to come to the phone, if I would like to try later . . .

Then there was a noise in the background, there was a disruption that obviously was setting the secretary aback. This was some kind of event she wasn't used to having to have to cope with. I knew instantly what had happened. Christopher hadn't remembered his letter. He had only registered a call from an unknown party in a far northern state where he wasn't used to doing business. He'd told the woman to get rid of me. But the connection between the source of the call and my initials — all I had identified myself with in the ad — had come to him and he had raced out to countermand his original order.

"He'll be right with you," the woman finally said.

"Yes," he answered not long after that. His voice was deep, almost too masculine to believe.

"I'm answering your letter, about the trip to California?"

"Yes, . . . sir." The sir was almost whispered, as though he still worried about the secretary hearing him. "I'm glad you called."

"Can you clear your schedule for the fifteenth? I'll come through your city and interview you."

"Interview me?" He was upset by that. "Is that really necessary?"

"I would think you'd enjoy it." I smiled at his discomfort and began to look forward to this little visit.

"Is it honestly an interview? Is the party still on?"

"Yes, yes," I answered. "You should also be prepared to fly to San Francisco. I'll see you on the fifteenth. If you're . . . appropriate, we can make the other arrangements. The party is on a Saturday night. You won't have to worry about missing too many days in your office if that's a concern."

"Hardly," he was laughing now. "I can't imagine why anyone would go all that distance for a single weekend. But I'm sure I can find some other ways to keep myself occupied out there — if it's necessary."

Ah, my Christopher was already looking for extra time and added activities.

"Are you sure that an interview is necessary, though? Didn't you see my pictures? Didn't you like them?" I wasn't surprised that any man as interested in his own body would be so confident that he would be admired and wanted. But that wouldn't be a proper way for us to proceed. We needed a more clear understanding of what was going on.

"As my ad stated, looks aren't enough. I have to know that you're appropriate for my purposes. That can't be ascertained without an interview, a try out, if you like."

"Well, . . ." he was riffling through some papers, checking his schedule, "yes, the fifteenth would be fine."

"This is something that should happen on my grounds, not yours." I gave him the name of a downtown hotel where I'd been before.

"Of course I know it, sir." I think he actually understood. "Can I ask . . . I would like to know what you look like, do you mind telling me . . ."

"Yes, I do. In any event, it's my money that I'm spending coming to your city. If you are only after a certain type of person — rather than a type of experience — then you can always leave me. There'll be no hard feelings. But, for now, I think it's better for you simply to arrive, without warning and without the usual bottom fantasies. Just prepare yourself for the test. I am not, after all, calling in response to a dating service."

"I'm sorry, sir. I didn't mean...," he was backtracking after hearing the anger in my voice.

"Enough. I'll write you with my complete name and other instructions later. I'll expect you to follow them to the letter."

"Of course. Of course I will. This is very exciting, sir, I can't thank you...."

"Don't, not now." With that I hung up.

* * *

I was sitting in the hotel cocktail lounge when I did finally meet him. He was nervous, of course. I had told him to come directly from his office and he must have; he was still dressed in his three-piece suit and his wing-tip shoes. I guessed that the costume was one of the last that he would have chosen to wear to meet a sexual partner, but I was delighted by it.

He sat down across from me after I had motioned to him and signaled that, yes, I was the one. He had received a letter with a fair description of myself. I had learned to make the descriptions I send to someone I'm meeting through the personal ads for the first time as inauspicious as possible. I only describe myself in terms that will encourage them to show up, never in ways to make them have high expectations. That way, they're invariably delighted with what they do find.

Christopher certainly was. The big smile on his face was full of delight and relief. He sat down across from me and a waiter approached. "A martini, straight up," he ordered. But I countermanded it.

"No, I've already ordered a bottle of Chablis. It's on ice now. That will do." I turned to the waitress, a very appealing young woman with firm breasts that weren't being restrained by a bra. "You could pour it now."

"Of course." She went to go and get the wine.

Christopher understood immediately that the little exchange between the three of us was meaningful. It set the limits immediately. He sat back in the lounge chair, the grin was gone, but not the enjoyment.

We didn't speak until the wine was brought, opened and poured. The waitress looked even better when she bent over to serve each of us. The management had forced her to wear one of those ridiculously short skirts and stockings with seams in them. I flashed on a fantasy of having both her and Christopher up to my room. They would make a fine couple together. But she left. I had him and certainly expected that he would be more than sufficiently engaging for this night at least.

He had dark hair, probably brown, but so deep that it could have been black. The lighting was so soft that I couldn't be sure. His muscles were developed enough that they were obvious even through the layers of clothes. His arms, especially, were so large at the biceps that they had presented the tailor with a special problem.

He was clean-shaven and actually had a small but noticeable cleft in his chin. His eyes were a dark shade — again the room's lighting didn't really let me see them but I thought they were also probably brown. While he dressed and carried himself in ways that he obviously hoped would make him appear older, there was a boyish quality about him, a mischievous manner when he studied me over the top of his glass and an ease with his body that contradicted its size.

He lifted his wine and toasted me silently, but then stopped before he drank. He remembered the situation and — very enjoyably — waited for me to give a signal. I picked up my own glass and nodded, and we both took a swallow.

"Tell me about yourself," I said.

He put the glass back on the table and studied me for a moment. "I'm not used to that, you know — talking about my . . . real life." He wasn't challenging me, nor was he playing a game. I understood. But I also knew something else.

"If you hadn't wanted to talk about yourself you wouldn't have written me on real letterhead and you wouldn't have been so calm about my coming to your home town."

"Perhaps." That was all he'd own up to.

"My question stands: tell me about yourself."

He took a deep breath. "You know my occupation. I'm fairly

successful. I'm married." He took another drink, as though wanting to punctuate that last statement. He was studying me again, wondering how I was going to deal with his disclosure. I didn't react.

He continued, "I live here, president of the Rotary, the youngest they've ever had. I am a member of the right church, Presbyterian in this town. I went to a local college, quarterback of the football team, president of my fraternity, ranked number one in graduate school..." He let his voice drop off and lifted his hands as if in defeat.

I knew the story. I'd heard it a million times. The man in charge, the one in control. He didn't have to tell me some of the details, I knew them by heart. He'd risen in his community by being everyone's ideal of the American male. He was decisive in business, a leader in small groups. His wife, without doubt, was one of those totally dependent types, the ones who loathe feminism and run from its implications. She, like all the others, would have chosen this man just for those attributes.

And, for him, there was no escape. The dirty little secrets of his adolescence had terrified him and sent him scurrying into a deep and forbidden cave where they were made safe. All of his extraordinary activities were compensation for those concealed realities.

He would be one of the hungry ones. The ones who present themselves with amazing needs. "Are you gay?"

He shifted a little bit, his eyes avoided me. "Not really. That's not what's important — it being a man or a woman. What's important is...," but he stopped, he seemed to understand where he was and to think that the confession was inappropriate.

I understood that as well. I stared at him for a minute before continuing, "What's important is that someone — anyone — take charge. That's it, isn't it? You just need someone to relieve you of the pressure of all those decisions, all those responsibilities."

"Yes." He was staring back at me. I couldn't find the emotion he was feeling.

I reached into the pocket inside my jacket and brought out a small black paper bag. "This is for you. Go to the men's room and put it on. It will help us make sure we both understand what's happening here."

He looked at the parcel sitting on the table and seemed to be terrified of it. It was defiling his safe space. He scanned the room, as though he might find a fellow church member or a Rotarian witnessing his sacrilege. But — of course — he finally picked up the bag and did as I had told him to.

He walked away as as though he were a busy man on a quick errand. He strode across the room and disappeared around a corner into the lobby. In only about five minutes he returned, but his walk was decidedly less jaunty and self-assured. I watched as he made his way across the cocktail lounge with careful steps.

When he sat down I told him, "Squeeze your hand into your lap, hard." I said it casually; no one looking at us could have seen anything strange about the way we were talking to one another.

As soon as he began to follow the single instruction, I added another one, "Put your legs together."

He was obviously obeying. He was struggling to keep the expression on his face from breaking into a grimace. The color had left his skin. There were a few beads of sweat gathering on his forehead.

"That's enough. Relax."

He couldn't hold back the comfort that came over him when he did. He opened his mouth wide, gulping for breath.

The package had contained a simple, but effective device. At first it appears to be just a cockring, a small leather band with studs on it. But on the lining, the studs are not closed: the sharp protrusions are open. They are — at the least — terribly uncomfortable. When pressure's applied, they bite into the skin painfully. That pressure, of course, is what he had felt when his hand was in his lap and his legs were pushed shut.

It has always been a favorite of mine. Especially for men who chose to wear costumes like Christopher's suit. If they want to project that image for the world, fine, let them, at least occasionally. But for me, just between the two of us, there should be something going on that is a constant and emphatic reminded of the roles we've chosen.

"May I" He was reaching for his wine glass and picked it up after I'd said yes. He needed that drink and proved it by draining his glass. The waitress appeared almost immediately and refilled it.

"I've cleared my schedule, as you told me to. There are lots of reasons for me to be in California. Actually I go there — supposedly on business — at least four times a year. No one's suspicious."

"But we haven't agreed that you should."

The cock ring was serving its purpose now. I'm sure he would have made some quick reply before he'd put it on. But now he was more aware of the possibilities and the repercussions of what was going on. "I hope you'll let me."

It was a perfect answer. "Tell me more about why you want to do it — this particular event."

He thought for a while. "I told you I was an athlete in college for one thing. But working out and not having a real physical outlet like the athletic field makes me more ... conscious of it.

"I spend my days aware of what I'm doing, developing my abdominals, expanding my chest, all of it. It has a strange repercussion I really hadn't expected. I had always liked having people watch me and like me and my body. But now, with the greater effort and the stronger focus on what things look like, I've discovered that desire is even stronger than I could ever have imagined.

"I want something more extreme. When I saw your ad and read the description, I knew that's what it was.

"You asked before what was important. I do — as I said — go to leather bars and I do have nights with men. Yes, answering the ad was a risk. But the ad itself gave me the courage and the trust. It was so ... elegant. I knew I wasn't dealing with any kind of street thug. It wasn't as though you were offering a gang rape. 'A private party for a very few invited ladies and gentlemen...' That's hardly an invitation to a cheap orgy.

"My private needs are almost completely segmented from my life. It allows me a great deal of freedom, actually. I can take the risk of your being here because I don't take any other risks. This is my hometown, of course, you're right about that. But I'm never found in the bars here.

"The homosexuality really isn't much of it at all. If I could find women who were as discreet as some of the men I know and if they knew how to fulfill my desires, I'm sure I'd be perfectly willing to do these things with them."

He had regained his composure and confidence with his

speech. I quickly thought I should put him back in his place, but instead I was distracted with the idea of just how very much Madame would like to get her hands on this one. She would have a field day putting him through his paces. The thought of her pleasure was enough to make me suspend my other criteria. Of course I'd have to have him at the party.

That didn't mean I couldn't have him now.

"Let's go to my room."

* * *

When we got there I took one of the two comfortable chairs by the picture window that overlooked the downtown area. I took out a cigarette and held it. It took him a moment to respond, but then he realized what I wanted and moved over to me. There were matches in the ashtray and he took them and lighted the smoke for me.

"Undress."

There was a momentary hesitation. Of course, I realized, he would have preferred that I do it. But I wanted to make sure he had the experience of taking off his clothes to a passive observer. It was a lesson he'd have to learn.

He went to the nearby closet and opened it. He took off his suit jacket and vest and hung them up. Then he undid his shirt. He bent over and began to unlace his shoes. A sharp frown swept over his face and I knew that the spikes in the ring had bitten into his balls. But he continued. He kicked the shoes into the closet. The shirt came off now and was also hung up. He seemed to hesitate again when it came time to unbuckle his belt. But the indecision was so fleeting that I didn't even have a chance to mention it. He stepped out of the trousers.

The socks and undershirt were next. Now he was standing there only in his tightly cut boxer shorts. He was already half erect; I could make out the lines of his cock through the fabric. Now he faced me. He pulled down the underpants and stood before me naked.

It was a fine sight. I realized, now that I was seeing him close up, that he shaved his body. There were only the slight hints of that — not a single hair outside a clearly defined triangle of his pubic region and under his arms. I knew that I would feel the stubble when I ran my hands over his chest.

He moved towards me. His cock was arcing out from his abdomen. It swung slightly as he moved, its base still entrapped by the black leather band. He moved until he was right in front of me. I reached up and circled my hand around the leather and applied enough pressure to make him wince. He loudly breathed in through his mouth and his body stiffened from the sharp pain.

I stood up. "Put your hands behind your neck. Spread your legs apart as far as you can. Hold your head up. Eyes front, immobile."

He immediately went into the stance I'd dictated. I walked around him, running my hand along the expanse of his body. It was a work of art. He'd suffered for it. I could only imagine the hours of exertion.

His back was as wide as it had looked in the photographs. I could feel ridges and valleys in his flesh that I had never seen so sharply defined in other men. I reached down to his buttocks and felt them. Amazing. They were as solid as most other men's arms. I could squeeze them and feel the resistance of the well-developed flesh. His thighs were thick, and rope-like structures of muscle wrapped around them.

I came around to the front. I could feel the unnatural smoothness of his shaven chest as soon as my palm touched his pectorals. His nipples were developed as well, but I knew their exercises had nothing to do with gymnasiums. I pinched one a little — nothing severe, just enough to elicit a satisfying response from him. His balls, too, were shaven.

"How do you explain this to your wife?"

"She thinks all bodybuilders do things like this. Probably. If she notices at all. We don't have an ... imaginative sex life."

His stomach was hard, with horizontal lines that displayed the sections as well as a textbook would. But, of course, the arms were the most appealing. The mass of his biceps was incredible.

The explorations I was making — and probably the distant manner with which I was making them — was turning him on incredibly. His erection had filled out as far as it could, the arc now lifted it straight up, as it appears in some of the ancient pictures of Pan, his cock pointing to the ceiling in a vertical bow.

The tip was circumcised — always a disappointment. But it was large, a thickly purple-colored and smooth-skinned prize on the end of a long and substantial shaft. I ran my fingers up and down its length, very gently. He closed his eyes when I did that, as though the very touch was a private and exquisite torture.

I moved away from him and took off my own clothes, simply draping them over my bed. When I was naked, I sat down on the chair again and spread my legs.

"Your knees."

He had been studying me and now stared, hesitating this time because he was trying to figure out the way I wanted him to arrange this maneuver. He did it correctly, keeping his hands behind his neck and his legs spread, he lowered himself into the space between my thighs.

He was going to move in to suck me at once. I put a hand on his forehead and stopped him. I reached for the small black pouch that I had earlier placed by the chair and pulled it up. I reached in and brought out a pair of rubber-tipped clamps. He knew what they were for and his eyes dropped down, as though he was surrendering to them.

I opened one of the clamps and put it on one of his nipples. They were firm, but not viciously painful. They would begin to be, but later, and only if I chose to leave them on for a period of time. I repeated the effort with the second clamp.

He was used to this, I was sure of that. But he wasn't used to the next step. I took out two small bells from the pouch. Each one was attached to a tiny ring which matched a small hook on the end of the nipple clamps. I put them on him, a quick and surprisingly effective means of letting him know that I had tricks and expectations beyond the usual ones that he had been accustomed to in the bars.

As soon as I let go, the two little bells rang softly. His eyes were wide open with amazement as he studied them, his careful reserve was gone and he was trying to understand that those sounds were being produced by his own body's movements.

Then he closed his eyes. His forehead tightened into a frown. His body actually seemed to shake slightly. Through clenched teeth he said, "I hate those — the bells."

I reached down and used my forefinger to tap one of them enough to create the sound again.

"You've spent all this time to create a body someone else would appreciate and you get upset just because he does something to make you even more handsome?" My finger moved to the other side of his chest and rang the second small bell.

He seemed to relax quickly. I could watch the tension leave his shoulders and his chest as the muscles softened. He wanted this so badly — he thought he needed this so badly — that he was willing to put up with the new humiliation.

"Put your hands down," I told him.

He did, and at the same moment opened his eyes. He didn't look at me, though. Instead he studied the silver bells that hung from his chest. His arms rested by his sides. His cock was still hard. No matter how much he protested the bells, he was still being tremendously turned on.

I went back into the pouch and pulled out a collar. It was plain leather, there were no spikes inside this piece. I held it up in front of his face. "You are the kind of man who needs this — the symbol — aren't you?"

He studied the leather and nodded, "Yes, sir." His voice was barely a whisper; the person who occupied his office and dominated his wife while impressing his community wouldn't be able to loudly acknowledge the desire for a collar, of course.

"Bend your neck." He did, quite nicely. I reached over and pulled the collar around the broad stalk. After I'd secured the buckle which held it in place, I sat back again. My cock was hard, it was resting up against my body. This time, when he looked up, the bells made no difference and the posture of submission wasn't so important. His eyes were focused only on my erection. He ran a tongue across his lips.

"What does that mean to you — the collar?" I asked. I was calmly stroking myself only inches from his face.

"That ... that I have no control. That I have to do what you say. That you are my master and I must follow your orders." He was speaking in that husky whisper again. The tone was nearly religious, he had undergone a spiritual transformation and whoever he was outside this room was no longer important. He was only a naked man on his knees, a collar around his neck, his cock hard, his body available.

I pulled out a wrapped condom and handed it to him. He studied it for just a moment, then went to work. He carefully opened the foil and pulled out the latex. He looked at me, silently requesting permission to continue. I nodded. He reached up and put the unrolled condom on the tip of my cock. Then, very slowly and very reverently, he pulled the thing down over my erection.

He worked at it carefully and methodically until the entire shaft was covered. Then he sat back on his haunches, still staring at my erection. The movement set the bells off again, but he didn't care at all, he hardly seemed to notice.

I reached down and took hold of the base of my cock. I milked it slightly until we could both make out the seeping precum as it was pressed up against latex. I pushed the erection away from me so it was pointed directly at him. "Suck it, carefully."

He moved very slowly towards his task. He opened his mouth inches before it was necessary. I was able to see the pink of the inside of his mouth. His teeth were white; hardly any evidence of correction could be seen. My adult athlete took in the head of my protected cock. But he was out to impress me. That, and he was out to savor the moment. He kept his jaw as open as possible, he had to have worked to relax his throat muscles. The whole length of me went inside him in the one, single movement he made.

The sounds were marvelous. I was looking down at him, fighting off the nearly overwhelming sensation of his hot mouth engulfing my cock, and watching his attempts, no matter how vain, to give pleasure. I could have remained that way for hours. If my cock were at least as disciplined as he was, that is.

But he moved back after a few seconds, not letting my cock free, his mouth was now wrapped tightly around the head. Through the latex I could feel his tongue moving over the surface of my tip. It was a grand feeling, but not so dangerous to me that I was going to lose control from it the way I might have if he had been able to continue to capture my cock in the depths of his throat.

I regained myself, feeling as though some kind of chemical rush had just passed through me and I was only now getting back a sense of my actual self. I quickly collected some thoughts. I reached down, leaning over him while his head kept moving ever so slightly at its task. "Don't you dare let it slip out," I said softly. It was unnecessary in one sense: He obviously wasn't anxious to let my cock go. But it worked in another: It made it clear that he was still in his role.

I took both my hands and went to his chest. I found the little bells and began to move them both at once, letting them play a duet between themselves. The motions must have created some real discomfort, if not actual pain. He began to twist a slight bit from side to side and low groans escaped from his chest. The sounds and the physical reactions were too real to have come only from his hatred of the bells.

I kept one hand moving on a bell and moved another down to his crotch, having to move so close to him that now the thick hair on top of his head was brushing against my own naked chest. I found him still rock hard and now dripping fluid. I grabbed hold of the thick shaft and roughly twisted first one way and then another. More, louder, groans came from him.

But it wasn't until I moved to the metal-lined cock ring and grabbed it that he really began to display the effects of pain.

His mouth opened wide and I felt a sudden draft of cool air where I had grown accustomed to the wet heat. He was gasping for strength and air. But he wouldn't move, I had to give him that credit. He stayed there, my rigid cock still in the center of his mouth. He overcame the pain and returned to his task, once again enveloping my erection in his throat. He wasn't going to give in quite so easily.

I released both my hold on his cock ring and on his bell and sat back. I studied him as he now returned to his task undistracted. His head was moving quickly, his tongue making its own movements to keep in sync with the thrusts he was creating. His hands were still at his side, but once he understood that I intended to remain passively enjoying the pleasures of his body, he moved them up to gently cup my testicles and hold them close to my torso.

The sight of his back was incredible. I saw all of the physical strength it contained. I could see his buttocks as they rested their meaty mounds on his heels. All of it was visually perfect. And all during it there was the sound of the small bells as they sent out the messages of his labor.

When I knew that his work was going to bring me to an orgasm soon, I pulled my cock from his mouth. He studied it, a lost look in his face while he saw it directly in front of his eyes. I had a hand on the back of his neck to hold him in place. Of course he could have used his power and freed himself from the embrace. But what he wanted, obviously, was to be free from the use of his power. That was his commonplace role — to be powerful. This was his fantasy — to be under some one else's control.

I guided his neck upwards. He wasn't sure at first what I wanted. But soon he knew that I expected to feel that tongue on my nipples. When the recognition came, he leapt to the duty. Somehow he knew that it was important that I feel the opposite of what he was experiencing. Instead of his teeth nibbling and applying pressure that might possibly come close to pain the clamps were giving him, he worked my nipples with great and deliberate care.

He seemed to be timing himself to my movements. As I came closer and closer to my orgasm, his mouth only worked more intensely. His head crossed back and forth over my chest, taking care of both nipples as well as he could.

I could feel the boiling in my groin as I started to come with the vision of the muscled executive on his knees in front of me. I ripped off the condom. Pressure crept up from deep inside and when it erupted, so did my cock, shooting out pulses of fluid all over his chest.

I pushed him back while I was still coming, wanting to see the spurts fly onto his shaven body, once even hitting one of the silver bells. Without any hair to impede their movement, the strings of stuff rolled down over him quickly. When my belly was empty and I had regained at least some of my breath, I reached over and used my palm to smear the seminal fluid all over his chest.

I sat back, looking at him. There was no hint of the respected businessman left. As I saw him now with his knees spread apart, his cock still erect, his torso showing the slightly white evidence of the rapidly drying come, he appeared to be just what he had presented himself as — a masochistic slave anxiously attempting to please his master.

"You do need this."

"Please, sir...," his voice trailed off as though he had been caught at something horribly embarrassing. He looked away from me. I leaned back over and grabbed his neck again.

"You do need this, don't you?"

He was there, collared and defenseless by his own choice. What could he say?

"Yes, sir." He hung his head back down.

"Come here, closer," I said, motioning him forward. He crawled the small space between us on his knees. I felt the contact with his still hard and now wet cock. I reached and again began to play with his bells. He closed his eyes again, the pain of the physical sensation and the humiliation were both merging. But the erection wasn't going away.

I moved my leg to the place between his thighs and ran my foot over the smooth skin. I lifted it up until I came into contact with his shaven scrotum. It was silky smooth; no other part of the body feels quite so perfect when shaved.

I rubbed my foot harder against him until it was again pressing the spiked cock ring into his flesh and eliciting the gasping sounds of his reaction.

"Put your hands back behind your head." He didn't hesitate to comply. "Now rub against me." I put my foot down on the floor as soon as I had said that.

He was puzzled. "Rub your cock against my leg until you come."

He lifted himself and pushed his erection against my shin, just below my knee. He began to move his hips to a silent cadence. I could feel the spongy flesh over the blood filled shaft as the skin stretched and retracted with his motions.

His armpits were open to me. They were strangely pale in comparison to the otherwise tanned chest and arms. Seeing the few thin wisps of hair seemed to make him even more vulnerable.

"You enjoy that, don't you?"

"Please, sir, let me just beat off," he asked. I shook my head no. He didn't stop his movement. "Please, take off the clamps. Stop the bells." No again.

His scrotum was swinging now and I could feel it bouncing against me every once in a while. The idea of masturbating against my leg was thrilling him and repulsing him. I knew that. But the thrill was dominating him. His cock was moving even more rapidly and the actions caused the bells to continue to ring.

His breath was coming more rapidly, his face was beginning to flush. "This is just the way you should be, collared, your body adorned, your cock hard while you beg a master to let you come."

"Yes, sir," he said.

"You'll come to San Francisco for nothing more."

"Please, sir, when I'm there, please don't make me wear the bells." He was honestly begging me.

"The only thing I promise you is this: When you come to San Francisco and undress for me, the first thing that will happen is that I will put these same bells on your nipples and you will go around my party with them on, letting the others know you're approaching with the sound, announcing that they can do anything to your nipples that they choose..."

And with that, he came against my leg.

Teaching

I read the letter while sitting on the plane as it soared away from Ohio.

Dear Sir:

I've probably already made my first mistake. I mean, with the way I addressed this.

It's not that I'm inexperienced in S&M, but I do know I don't understand all the "right" ways to do things. If that makes any sense to you.

I'd better get to the basics before I fuck this whole thing up. I'm 22. I'm enclosing a couple recent snapshots of myself so you can see I'm not bad looking. I'm short, only about 5'6". I hope that doesn't bother you. I'm a student at a local university — studying to be an electrical engineer.

I come from Colorado. I grew up in a small town a distance from Denver. I've been gay as long as I can remember — and very active.

It started when I was young. As far back as I can remember, I was trying to get the other kids to take off their pants. Most of it was the usual stuff. But I got into some things that you'd probably call S&M early on as well.

The other guys and I would play wild games. Our version of cowboys and Indians was a lot more authentic than what I hear other guys say they did when they were growing up, that's for sure.

We Coloradans know that the cowboys and the Indians tied one another up and tortured one another — all the time. I used to always try and figure out which side was the weakest so I could join it and have the best chance of being captured.

This went on until I left home to come to school here in Denver. By the end, a bunch of us had the game down to a science and the science we were studying didn't end up with just a few rope tricks.

That was all just pretty hot teenage fun, though. I never was in any real S&M scene, just these really rough things with the kids back home.

I've been going to the gay bars here in Denver ever since I arrived in town. The stuff I get into here is . . . okay. I've met some nice guys and I've even had a fling or two that lasted a while. But there's no way to find people who are interested in the rough stuff that I knew at home.

I've always wanted to get back into it. There are some leather bars here, of course. But they don't do it for me. I don't understand all the lingo and the handkerchief codes and that. The discos I usually go to are just kiss and suck dating places.

I am planning a vacation in San Francisco. I was thinking that maybe the classified ads would give me a way to get into some new adventures. That's when I saw your ad. My problem is that I'll just be arriving in the city when your thing is going on. I can't get there any earlier. Is there any way to get an earlier interview? Or maybe we could just get together — you and me — after that's done with?

I began by saying I was sorry. I just don't know all the words and I can tell from what I read that they're important. I don't mean to be disrespectful or stupid. But no one's taught me anything yet.

Well, not that kind of stuff, anyway. I remember being tied up by the guys at home and I remember how much it turned me on. There's a lot going on inside my head about it. It's what I think about when I go on "nice" dates with "nice" guys and we play like we're never going to do anything like "that." If you know what I mean.

I suppose I'm just fresh to everything. I don't know if that bothers you very much. All I can say is I'll try very hard to do the right thing.

I'm so uneasy about it all because what you talked about in the ad is so ... structured, I guess.

It sounds like you only want a pro who would be able to understand all of it. But, like I said, I'll try. And I want to try. It sounds like you're into some strange things, but they sound hot to me!

Your friend,
Keith

I folded the letter and put it back in my jacket pocket. I still held the photograph. I didn't have to worry about looking at it in front of my fellow passengers. If any happened to see the picture there was no possibility of them thinking there was anything nefarious about it.

It showed a very attractive young man. Actually, he looked cute. I seldom use that word, but it applied to Keith. He was standing in a pair of crisp, possibly ironed, jeans and a polo shirt. He was smiling directly into the camera. He was an icon of American clean-cut youth. And he wanted to be a servant at an S&M party.

One of the most ridiculous protests people make about those of us who explore erotic fantasies is the claim that our activities are products of the decadent city, as though they could only be produced by members of the urban subcultures.

My life in northern New England proved that was a sham. The men there are often like Keith. They might not know the precise meaning of the symbols that the urbanites have developed in order to communicate with themselves, but they understand the lightning of harsh sexuality stripped of social pretensions.

Keith's letter resonated with the stories I had heard in other places. I would have been attracted to his open approach in any event, but the picture, with those wide and smiling eyes and the promising curves of his jeans, made him enough of a priority to justify a stop on my way to California.

I had talked to him on the phone a few times after receiving his letter. The openness, the sense of excitement and wonder — and certainly, the horniness — were all in his voice. There was no changing his schedule, college dictated that. But I could create this opportunity to spend a night in Denver. We could have our interview then.

The plane continued on, the steward served drinks. What a shame that they're forced to wear such formless clothes — not even room for a hint of chest hair to creep over the collars of their shirts. Their plastic smiles are so unmoving and so lacking in emotion.

I thought about the waste these stewards and their female counterparts stood for. They were forced to be automatons, deceived into thinking they were professionals because they had a union and rights and contracts. They were only servants, simply and purely. How much more pleasure we all would have gotten if they had been willing to assume that proper role. The flight from Ohio to Colorado was over two hours long. There was more than enough time in there for some amusement with one or another of them if they weren't protected by their ideas of their places in society. Their airline would reap untold increases in profits and they could collect fine gratuities if they only understood better what their customers wanted and would be willing to spend for.

But the deceptions go on in many different arenas.

Christopher rankled me. That was part of it. The idea of him — his incredible body and his perfect masochism — were all intensely pleasurable. I wasn't going to complain about that nor deny it. I would have him at the party and I would possibly have him to enjoy later on as well. But it would only be a masturbatory thrill. He would present only that body of his, there would be nothing else.

"Love?" No, I haven't used that term. I certainly wouldn't use it in relationship to Christopher. I didn't want anything like that from him. But there could have been more content, something to make the pleasure of that perfect body even more intense. There are so many sexual connections that can be made between men — between people — that can have so many benefits and include so many planes of experience, that accepting only the physical seems insufficient. Would I have accepted Christopher's limitations if he hadn't been so handsome? If his body hadn't been so perfect?

The segmentation he had constructed, and which he gave every indication he was going to hang on to, was the same that Keith was trying to avoid. Sex as revolution has its own appeals to me. I smiled as I thought of myself sitting in the first class compartment of the American Airlines jet and conceiving of myself as a revolutionary. But there were ways in which it was valid to think of that.

Adrienne says it is my duty to change the course of Western Civilization. I! With my sexually ostentatious parties and my first person paeans to male beauty? I don't think so. I certainly don't plan my life on it. But, as I looked at Keith's photograph still one more time, I decided it would be quite wonderful to change the course of his personal life history. My little Keith wouldn't be stuck in suburban discos with wistful memories of cowboys tying him to trees in preparation for exquisite tortures — not when I was done with him, at any rate.

* * *

I had Keith meet me in the hotel dining room. I purposely chose it because of its elegance. It is one of the finest in the west, known not only for the cuisine, but also for the extraordinary service.

He had told me that he'd never been here. In fact, it appeared he'd never been to a fine restaurant of any kind anywhere. His concept of a meal "out" was a steak house. I was appalled by that. There had been a time when the entrance into gay life had been a ticket to great social mobility. A young gay man who had been denied a social education could find many men, not all of them necessarily older, who would trade the appreciation of his body for the lessons in social conduct and knowledge that would allow him to move in the world.

Those were not mere hustlers — though I'm sorry to imply that male prostitutes should ever be described as "mere" anything, at least by definition. They were young men whose birth had handed them the accident of membership in the lower classes — whose existence we are supposed to ignore. That we live in a democratic society is one of the great lies of America.

At least, once upon a time, being gay meant being freed from those restrictions. Now, with the superficial elements of "acceptance," our young men are sucked into the belief that they're like everyone else. Who ever told them that was desirable? To be like everyone else in America is to be ruled by television, to sublimate desire, to believe that a franchised steak house is the height of gastronomic delight.

If I gave Keith nothing else this trip, I would introduce him to the hotel dining room and let him have at least one experience with a waiter who saw his job as something more than a way station in life. Here, I knew, the staff would be delighted with their positions, honored to be a part of the traditions that existed in this hall.

I sat in the cocktail lounge and waited for him. He was a little early. I had warned him that there would be severe repercussions if he was late. I had refused to describe myself. He didn't know who he was meeting and I enjoyed the few moments while he floundered, wondering whether or not to have a drink, hesitating twice as he moved towards the bar.

I finally stood and motioned for him to join me. His face lit up when he realized who I was. He seemed to bound across the room rather than simply walk. He had the energy and the enthusiasm of youth — a wonderful combination.

"Hello," he put out his hand. I purposely didn't take it, only looked down at it. "Oh," he said softly, "is that a mistake? Aren't I supposed to do that? I'm sorry."

But I did grab his hand and accepted his greeting. "I'm glad to meet you, Keith. Have a seat."

He was wearing a worn blue blazer. It was probably the same one he had purchased for his graduation party in high school. His slacks were old and scuffed, certainly not the height of fashion. But I could tell he'd tried hard to iron a crease into them and the effort was more appealing than the vast majority of final products would have been. His shirt was also freshly ironed. The tie was knotted unevenly. His hair was slightly too long, not in terms of fashion, just in the fact it needed to be cut. He had done battle with a cowlick that had defeated him and which, probably without his knowing it, was sticking in the air at the back of his head.

All in all? A delightful picture.

I had made certain arrangements with the maitre d' and we went directly into the dining area. Keith followed me as we were led through the well-dressed diners. I didn't even bother to ask what he thought of the extraordinarily high ceilings, the thick rug, the armies of waiters and busboys that moved so silently and efficiently through the room. If he had never been in such a place before, he was certain to be awed by it.

It took him a minute to realize that there was only one menu when we were seated at the table — mine. "I guess they forgot . . ."

"No, they didn't. I'll order for you."

"Fine," he said softly. He had the sense to sit silently while I read through the offerings. Water was poured, I ordered us wine, and then went over with the waiter the various foods that we'd eat, all the while refusing to speak to Keith. I simply chose for him what I, myself, was going to have.

I began the conversation over paté. "This is, after all, an interview." Just to keep him off guard, I added, "It's cost me a great deal of money to arrange this for you. I would like to know what it is that you have to offer me that will make this worth my time, and make it worth my time to include you in my party."

He was startled. "I . . . I sent you my pictures."

"A body isn't enough. A body can be had easily in many ways with many people. I want to know more about those attributes you have that make you think you're appropriate for my party."

"It doesn't seem like that's the question." There was a little insurrection brewing inside Keith, his back was stiffened and he spoke more loudly than he had before. "After all, you're the one who wants free labor for his party. I mean, come on, you expect . . . I don't know what you expect me to do. It doesn't seem like I'm the only one making the application."

"But you are," I smiled. I picked up my wine glass and sipped it. "I am the one who can offer you your fantasy. My fantasy is easily achieved. It isn't going to be difficult to hire a few professionals if I must. Obviously I could arrange that. But I am investigating letting you and a few others live out your dreams.

"I may not be playing cowboys and Indians like your childhood friends, Keith, but I certainly am arranging an event that will have more consequence than a night in your disco."

He let his head droop a bit. It was a very pleasant sight. "Tell me about it, please, the party, I mean. Tell me what it is you want. You've only talked around it. If I knew what was going on, maybe I could tell you why I'm the right one for it."

That was better, much better, I thought.

"The party will be private, as I said. There will only be four guests. In attendance will be an assortment of young men — all attractive. They will be the servants, obviously, some of them will be bringing on the food, pouring the drinks, that kind of thing. Naked. Of course. Then there will be others who will be the decoration. They will be assembled in various ways, bound, I suspect. I haven't decided those details. But they will be a part of the atmosphere of the gathering.

"The only absolute thing — and I promise you this much — is the privacy of it. There will only be the four guests, and there will be no photographs, no intrusions, no surprises. Of course there'll be nothing that would in any way harm you over any period of time. No permanent marks, no injuries, no drugs that might produce psychosis, far from it. I doubt you'll have more than a glass of wine, if that.

"The party will be very low key. It will last only a couple hours on a Sunday afternoon. Then it will be over. All of it. You will have had your experience. I will have had your obedient participation. I'm offering you this trade — my ability to create a moment you will remember for the rest of you life in return for your being a part of the stage set I am creating. Is that clear enough?"

"But what are the requirements? I mean, how can I interview for something like that if you want more than my body?" He was puzzled and I had no intention of not responding to his honesty.

"You can tell me what you have to offer. Why would you make a good servant? I'll examine your body later this evening to make sure it's all you claim and your photograph displays." He stiffened again; the idea that the interview would be sexual had only been implicit up to this point. "But your attitude is more important than anything else. Tell me about you. Why is it that those cowboy and Indian games reverberate through your memory?"

The arrival of our entree gave him a moment to collect his thoughts. He played with his food for a short while, studying it as a diversion. "I just liked it," was all he could come up with.

"There must be more to it than that."

"It made me feel ... alive. That's all." He stared directly into my eyes now. "It just seems that sex should be more fun than it is with most of the guys I know. It should have more to it." He looked back down and blushed. "I'm a really horny guy. I used to think that I was sick or something, I jerk off all the time.

"I have this ... appetite for sex. I want it whenever I can get it. I read the stuff about how it was before the health thing and I know I'd be on the first bus to New York if it was still that way. Man, the idea that there are places were you could get it on two, three, four times a day!

"I do my work, go to school, keep everything in order and that's all fine. But sex, man, sex is what makes life worth living.

"You know, I don't think it's that big a deal that what you're offering is S&M. That's one of the things I was hesitant about in answering your letter. I mean, it's fine, it's great, but I don't think I'm into it. I think I want to do it because it's sex. Anything that has to do with sex that I can do, I want it. I want it to be hot and I want to know what it's like.

"I do think about the cowboy and Indian thing, that was no lie. But I think about circle jerks and I think about the guys in the locker room and I think about construction workers and I think about . . . If it has a cock attached to it, I think about it."

He stopped his miraculous speech for a moment and seemed to soften as he looked at me now. "I think you understand. I used to think I was sick, you know, wanting to answer ads and wanting to go to parks and dreaming about cock all the time. No one else was talking about it, even in the bars. They were talking about all this other stuff — the love thing and all. But I think about it all the time.

"I'm not stupid. I know I'm not smart, but I'm not stupid. I did some reading, I forced some of the men I knew to talk to me. I discovered that I wasn't sick. I just had this overactive sex drive.

"So what am I going to do with it? I can't turn myself into a dream stud. I can't just add inches on to my height. I'm who I am. It's just that who I am is perpetually horny. That's why I'm going to San Francisco. I know, I know, I can't do it the way they used to, but I can see things, I can watch, I can be in places and I can jerk off till the end of time.

"So there's your ad. It just told me that there was a sex thing that was going on that was different than anything else I could experience. Go for it, I decided. I answered your ad.

"Does that make you angry? That I'm not totally into the S&M thing?"

"Hardly. The . . . enthusiasm for sex overwhelms that. I'm delighted with what you've said. For one thing, you've indicated that you're not opposed to what you so drolly call 'the S&M thing.' So long as you respect it, how you use it in the rest of your life isn't of interest to me."

Keith started up again, "I don't want to be boring. That's the big thing. I mean, look at me, I've got blond hair and blue eyes. I'm short. No one ever notices me. I smile a lot in bars. I'm just like every other American kid. That bothers me. I want to do something exciting. Like you said, I want to have an experience that I'll remember for years after. Of course, I'll do everything you want. I promise that."

"We'll see, Keith, as soon as we finish our coffee."

* * *

When we got to my room I took him by the back of his neck and dragged his face to mine for a long kiss. He responded beautifully, wrapping his arms around my shoulders and using them to lift himself up to my greater height. He made no resistance when I began to undress him.

The skin on young men is so smooth, so perfectly wonderful to touch. I've always regretted the years of my own youth when I didn't realize what I had and thought the sleekness of my flesh was an ordinary event. That kept me from truly appreciating this sensation.

I lingered over it. My hands swept his back and played with the waistband of his pants for a long time. I moved my palms over to the front of him, still holding on to his neck and with my mouth now gnawing on the front part of it. I could feel the hard roundness of his chest. There wasn't any discernible nipple to my feel. I knew — and I would be proven correct — that there hadn't been nearly enough attention paid to that part of his anatomy. Until this evening, at least. The clothes dropped away until I had to let him go to take care of the pants caught around his ankles and the shoes and socks that are always so awkward.

I left him to the embarrassing tasks and sat on the edge of the bed to watch him. When he stood up he was still wearing his jockey shorts. He moved to take those off as well, but the sight was too precious to allow that to happen. "No. Leave them on. Come back here."

He had, I'm sure, expected some kind of violent and rapid action. He had probably fantasized about a rape psychodrama — that's always the easiest thing to imagine in an assignation such as ours. But the circumstances were dictating my own response. Here was this small and adorable young man in his shorts, his hard cock poking a humorous bulge through the cotton fabric. His hair was already more tousled than it had been and his face was red and looked even younger. I couldn't pass this up.

I pulled him harshly towards me. He was again on my lap. I kissed him more. My hands went to the seat of his shorts and felt the firm flesh underneath. He squirmed from it and the little movements were beautiful indeed.

My hands moved under the crotch of the shorts and found his tight little balls captured in their sac. His cock was remarkably large in proportion to the rest of him; I could feel that from the base. I moved my hand around and grasped hold of it through the briefs. The tip had already wet the fabric.

He was moving wildly now, the very touch of my hand goading him on. He even began to moan a little bit. I moved my head down away from his mouth and neck and onto his chest. The nipples were, in fact, flat. They were barely pink colored and there was no definition of the center at all. They were lovely. My tongue ran across them and I discovered that even if they weren't well trained, they were certainly very sensitive.

My teeth nibbled. Keith's reaction let me know that there was little pleasure in that. But he was in his place, he was acting as though he understood that this was the deal that had been chosen by him. He wouldn't fight it. I kept up my teething just long enough to let him know his protests weren't the reason for my finally stopping.

Then I pulled down the back of the shorts and exposed the ass. A slight blond down covered them. I was surprised that there was a thick line of hair in the crack of his buttocks. I let one of my fingers probe the crevice. He began to squirm with renewed vigor. I let my finger press harder at the ring of muscle in the center of his body and there was a much louder and more emphatic sound coming from him than there had been before.

When my finger slipped past the protection and felt that perfect warmth of the inside of a male body, Keith began to really move. I forced the finger to continue moving deeper. My mouth was wandering pleasantly over his upper torso, just enough to keep all of his body in play.

Where was my mind? I was in such a state of utter enjoyment that I wanted to remember, but not enough to draw me away from it all. I conjured up a picture of a sultan with a young slave boy to play with. He was beautiful, all the slave boys would have been, and his cock was irrelevant. What was perfect was just this, just the simple fingering of his asshole and the wriggling he was involuntarily doing. It could only be that, he wouldn't dare attempt to escape. He wouldn't want to escape — being owned by this sultan would be the epitome of his dreams and desires. His only hope was to continue to make the sultan happy.

Keith was doing it and he was doing it awfully well. I gently moved our bodies to place his face down on the bed, then I slipped out from underneath him and directed his face upwards. My finger never left its sheath and the picture with which I was eventually rewarded was unforgettably perfect.

Keith buried his head in the covers. His unflawed back was a wave of young muscles leading down to his waist. His ass appeared even more rounded and more pronounced than it had felt. The soft hair on it was so slight it could hardly be seen. My finger kept up its probing and his wriggles increased with my motions, highlighting the curvature of his buttocks and producing occasional glimpses of dimples in the muscles.

Even the sight of the shorts gathered around his hips in wrinkles was perfect. He appeared only a young man being caught in something and the mixture of his unwillingness and his submission was right there in the indelicate shape of the shorts.

"Please, I'm going to come," he whispered. I could barely hear him, his voice was muffled by the bed cover.

"Don't," I warned. But I could imagine that the actions were too intense for him to be able to hold back. I didn't need to drive him to do something he couldn't control simply for an excuse to punish him. I already intended to do that. I slipped my finger out and left him sprawled out on the bed. I went into the bathroom to wash up and undress. When I returned I discovered that he'd turned down the lights. The room was subdued now.

Keith was on the bed, but this time he was face up. His hard cock was resting on his belly. His smaller balls were visible through the pubic hair; their excitement had lifted them up. His legs were spread apart to make sure I had a decent view. I wondered if he had consciously planned this exposure. He couldn't have done it any better if he had.

He smiled when he saw me and that I was naked. He lifted up his hands, as though expecting me to get on to the bed with him. Instead, I moved to the side and looked down at him. "Turn back over."

He did.

"Lift up your midsection."

He hesitated a bit, but then moved his legs up so his ass was raised to a better view.

"Spread your legs apart. I want to see in between them."

His thighs moved and I could see directly into the crack. His small hole, where I'd just been doing my exploring, seemed too little to have accommodated even my finger. It was a sudden brown color after the paleness of his skin. His balls seemed bigger now that I could view the whole length of his sac. I love the line of hard flesh that dissects testicles and the way that it travels all the way from the anus around to the beginning of the cock. I reached between his legs and pulled the half-erect penis back. I tugged hard enough to make sure he had a sensation that it was being pulled for an inspection and not some little romantic ploy.

I released it and then ran a hand on the smooth back. His shoulders rested on the mattress, and his head was turned so he could look back at me. I could see an excitement in his view. Part of it was just the idea of being exhibited this way, I was sure of that. But part of it was the expectation as well.

I wasn't about to disappoint him. With my left hand, I reached down around his waist and took a firm hold of his cock and balls in one grasp. They would be my handle. My right hand was free. I lifted it up while he watched in silence and let it smack down on first one, and then the other of his cheeks.

He took the first few strikes quietly, as though the fact of them was so interesting that he didn't feel them. But after a half dozen or so, when the skin was beginning to take on a pinkness, he began the same squirming that had greeted my fingering of him before.

I had no intention of stopping this pleasure and only tightened the grip on his genitals. They were a perfect anchor. My hand flew back and forth, first one side, then the other. I would alter the order just enough to keep him from ever being able to know where it would land.

I could feel the tingle spread over my palm as the speed and force of the blows increased. He moved his head and his arms. He was fighting against the pain and the sensation. He had picked up the pillow at the top of the bed and buried his face in it. I heard louder sounds from him and then — after one particularly unexpected and hard slap — he reared up, his face freed from the pillow, and he yelled out.

Whatever he said was incomprehensible. It was just the physical response to what he was experiencing. I ignored it. I kept up the attack, watching the skin grow a deeper and deeper shade of pink until there were ovals of dark red occasionally. My hand was stinging now. I tried to ignore it. I thought of taking my belt out and using that instead but stopped myself. It wouldn't deliver the pleasure this was creating and Keith might need to be brought slowly and carefully to that — the devices, no matter how simple, are always more frightening to the novice.

Then I stopped. I discovered that I was breathing with great difficulty. I had exerted myself immensely in the beating. My result was handsome. I still held Keith's cock and balls. There was no erection left. There was only the still upraised ass with its new rainbow of decorations. These are the moments I do want to have a camera, to capture the beauty of those marks. It would have been a memento worth having.

I released him carefully, letting his body slump onto the bed. His head was back in the pillow. I ran my hand up to the back of it and caressed him gently. I sat down now and both my arms went around his chest and pulled him up slowly. He'd been crying, his eyes were swollen and red and his whole face was damp.

As soon as I had taken him away from the emotional guard of the pillow, Keith gave up his defenses. His arms swept up and wrapped themselves around my neck. I'm not sure what his emotions were. Was he relieved it was over? Was he embarrassed that he was crying? Was it that I'd broken some barrier and therefore, since I had taken something away, I had to be trusted? Or was he just appreciative of what had happened? Such answers aren't easy to get at in the moment of the event. I didn't try to explore them.

I returned the embrace. His smooth-skinned body against my own chest hair was a lush sensation. He finally lifted up and began to languidly kiss my cheeks, then my eyes. The movements were slow, deliberate, almost adoring. They were clearly an invitation to continue the lovemaking.

I reached down and discovered that his cock had resuscitated itself. Once again, it was a hard silky capsule. I held it tightly and began to stroke it. But this, I decided, wasn't the way I wanted to end. I moved him again, back onto the bed facing me. My own cock was hard as well, and it was just as needy as his.

I stood in front of him, forcing a place for myself between his knees so that his thighs were spread far apart. I began to stroke both of us. I did it so the motions were in harmony, both of our cocks building toward their orgasm. He laid there, his hands moving over his own body, gliding over his chest, down to his belly, cupping his balls, while my movements continuing.

I felt the pressure build in me. My breathing was coming faster and deeper. His own rib cage was moving as well, swelling beautifully and then collapsing, making him appear older and his body more mature than it had ever before.

My balls began to move, they were pulsing with me now, the final announcement that an orgasm is really approaching. I stared intently into Keith's face. I heard him softly encouraging me on. I felt his cock stiffen even more and then it seemed that every muscle in my body contracted for one split second. A wave of energy swept through me. Everything was suddenly focused in my balls. Everything stopped quickly and suddenly, and then, just as suddenly, it erupted out of me as the fluids all rushed downwards and then out in pulsing waves.

I felt — just at the last moment — Keith's cock sharply rebel against my hand. Then, while I was still consumed with my own body's reactions, I barely began to understand that there was another source of wetness and warmth, that it was shooting out from him.

I collapsed on top of him while he was still coming, I could feel that hard young cock pumping stuff between us and I was only aware of one slight sorrow — that it would cool and we would be finished with this moment much too soon.

The Place

I had chosen an old hotel near Nob Hill, neither in the seediness of Union Square nor the elegance of the summit. It had seen decidedly better days, but those days had been glorious. The rooms were much larger than the cubbyholes that the modern chains provide, thinking that a spare phone in a bathroom or a mint on a pillow case can make up for space.

In its days this place had been grand. You could still see that in the height of the ceilings in every room, from the lobby to the closets. The old rugs were still there, threadbare in many places, but in corners where there'd never been too much traffic, the rich reds and yellows of the design could be appreciated.

The lobby had an extravagant waste of space. Large columns cut up the huge room and the corridors were wide enough for a small army to march up and down in parade formation.

I had reserved the largest suite. The desk clerks weren't used to people coming to the hotel in style any longer and I could see from their eyes that it had been ages since any one had purposely taken the "Presidential Suite." Certainly the cheap hustlers and prostitutes who were loitering on the lobby furniture weren't any indication that people were spending large amounts of money to stay here. It was hardly a place that a traveling salesman would choose to impress his clients or a visiting starlet the press.

I had my reasons for staying here. The hotel — like so many others in dying downtowns — had decided that it could resurrect itself with gay business and conspicuously advertised itself in gay newspapers and magazines. The manager, staff and — I was told — even the owners were gay and more likely to understand a variety of "special" needs.

The bellboy who carried my bags up to the room certainly seemed anxious to fulfill some of those needs. His tight rear was captured in pocketless trousers that accentuated his charms — both front and rear. He seemed to be Hispanic with olive skin, slick black hair and brown eyes. He would normally not be of interest to me. There was no indication his willingness extended to my personal proclivities, but his beauty was beyond doubt and the flirtatious manner with which he carried himself was endearing.

I toyed with the idea of picking up on his not so subtle messages while he showed me through the suite. The sitting room was perfect. I was so pleased that I almost forgot he was there. It was made for my circus. I was stunned by it. The ceilings were easily fifteen feet high. There were large, nearly floor-to-ceiling windows looking out over the city. Small pillars, not unlike the larger ones in the lobby, guarded the entrance to the room. The furniture was in disrepair, but some was obviously the original stuff the old hotel had used.

The rug was just as threadbare as the one downstairs, but it was enormous, nearly covering all the floor and only occasionally showing bits of parqueted wood. There were three couches, one against each wall — the wall that contained the entrance was the one without. Two armchairs stood in the corners between the couches. There were utterly horrible but ornate fake paintings on the one wall that didn't contain either a window or the entrance. They were drab, but appropriately set off by the long dingy painted walls.

A large cocktail table, nearly six feet long, sat in the middle of the collection of other furniture. My mind took in the space, the perfectly oversized furniture and the hint of history in the suite and I was overwhelmed by possibilities. Things had happened in this room that must have been extraordinary. The hotel had to have been built immediately after the earthquake and would by now have collected over eighty years of stories.

And I would add another.

I was extraordinarily pleased.

"Don't you want to see the rest?" The bellboy had to break

into my reverie to get my attention.

"Of course," I smiled to him and followed down the corridor.

"Sorry, the light's out here. I'll get someone up to fix it right away. It's not too dark, though. I mean, all the light from the other rooms is enough. But you should have lights. All this will get fixed soon enough. You know they're going to renovate. Man, this old place is going to be a lot different when they get done."

"Done? Who's going to do it?"

"One of them big companies, you know, with hotels all over the world. We're going to have to join a union, it's so big. But they're going to invest lots and lots of money into this place and make sure it's just as nice as the other ones around here. It's going to be something."

I was sure it was going to be another disgrace, another pile of little boxes for little businessmen and women to sit in while they did their little commerce in a society that was losing all of its sense of scale and majesty. I was having my party none too soon.

We went into the master bedroom next. This room was nearly as large as the other and was dominated by a large bed with tall and outlandishly decorative posts at all four corners. There were two more, smaller stuffed chairs. Again, a worn rug. The night tables that stood on either side of the bed didn't match. But the mirrors that stood at the head and across the room from the foot of the mattress were extraordinary. I studied them both and must have been smiling.

"Yeah, lots of guys, they like the mirrors. They can be pretty kinky." The young man was smiling lewdly as he watched me. The trousers weren't hiding anything; I could easily make out the lines of not only his cock but also his balls through the black cloth. He stood in the center of the room facing me and seemed to turn his head in a slight, seductive manner. Yes, of course he'd know how "kinky" those mirrors could be.

When I didn't respond, he seemed disappointed. His salary was probably minimum wage and the tips in a run-down hotel wouldn't have earned him all that much more. He probably needed the extra money that a trick could bring him. But I wasn't about to squander myself on a bellboy when I had so very much waiting for me here in San Francisco.

He took the clue and went about his business of placing my

bags on stands and then showing me into the bathroom. It was another treasure. It was tiled completely in white with only a very few black panels to create a pattern here and there. The toilet, the washstand and the tub were all old porcelain. The tub and the washstand were much larger than expected in hotels these days. The floor was the same tiles as the wall. Everything was in perfect condition, as though the materials had been of such good quality when the place was built that they could easily withstand the neglect they'd received since then.

The only indication of the age and disrepair of the building, itself, was the heat. The steam pipes were noisy, they'd already actually banged a couple times in the few minutes I'd been in the suite. That seemed a minor problem in the midst of all this and it did, at least, indicate that there would be heat. It was pleasant weather outside, and if the rooms became too hot I could simply open the windows and cool off that way.

"Sure you don't want anything else?" The bellboy's voice had a new tone in it. He actually sounded hurt, as though the rejection of his sexual services implied much more than I meant it to. I simply wasn't interested.

But he wouldn't leave, even when I hadn't responded. "I, uh, get off pretty soon. If you want anything, I can come back..."

"Not today. But I would like to have a special housekeeping done. I want it to be spotless. Can you arrange for a crew? I don't expect the staff to do the extra work on hotel time. I can see you're not paid for that. But I want this place in the best shape it's ever been. I'll pay for it."

I opened my wallet and took out a ten dollar bill as a sort of earnest money. He grabbed it quickly and studied it for a moment. "Sure, a couple maids, me and another guy to do the heavy stuff, it'll cost, a couple hundred bucks?"

"Fine."

His surprise showed that he had only been testing me. I could have gotten the job done for less. It certainly must have created the impression that I had unlimited wealth — which I don't. He warmed to me considerably.

"Hey, we'll have this place in great shape. We'll come in at ten in the morning, okay? Be done in a couple hours. You won't recognize it. We can get the best stuff out of the storeroom for you, make sure your towels are new and things like that. I'll tell my sister to take special care of you — she's a chambermaid. You'll see. You'll be glad you did this, man.

"What is it, you throwing a party? Or you got some big client coming here or something?"

"A party."

"Hey, you know, we can work it for you. We do that a lot. I can bartend, my sister can carry a tray of food, make it look like a real class act."

I tried to picture him and his sister naked at my party, with matching sets of metal earrings on their nipples. I smiled at the thought.

He mistook my humor. He thought he might have another chance now. "Hey, you interested in some ... very special service?" He groped himself openly. His hand forced his cock and balls into a tight knot that bulged obscenely — and quite nicely — in those black slacks of his. He moved closer.

The idea was becoming more appealing, I have to admit. He had a wonderful, fresh odor about him. His hair, especially, smelt clean and attractive. He was only a few feet away when I shook my head, no.

"Sorry," he shrugged. "You know, most of the guys who stay here..."

"Oh, I know. And I certainly know you're attractive. I'm simply not in the mood."

"Sure," he smiled, a little unconvinced. "But keep me in mind if you do get ... in the mood. My name's Joseph. You can ask for me at the desk if you want."

He began to leave. I felt a stirring in my crotch. I thought of a wonderful idea. "Wait."

He turned around. I had taken out my wallet again. "Just in case I do have the urge, I think I'd like to see what I'm going to buy." I handed him two more bills.

He took them and frowned. "Just to see?"

"Just to see," I assured him. I sat down in one of the chairs in a relaxed posture. "You needn't undress completely. Just drop your pants to your knees and lift up your shirt above your chest."

He hesitated for a moment, but then looked back down at the money I'd handed him. It was, I'm sure, as much as most men offered him for much more complex sex acts. He shrugged. After stuffing the bills in a shirt pocket, Joseph unbuckled his trousers and unzipped his fly. The slacks were so tight that he had to push firmly to get them down over his hips. He was wearing a pair of bright yellow underpants. There was no fly and their shape made his genitals appear much larger than I was sure they were.

He moved to push them down as well. His cock was half hard and arced out from his belly to point downwards. It was darker than the rest of his skin, almost a chocolate brown. His testicles were large and had the same dark color. The pubic hair was a thick web against his white abdomen.

Then he took the bottom hem of his shirt and lifted it up. His body hair was sparse above the waist. His stomach was flat and hard looking. His navel had a protrudence of flesh, a little nub, that stuck out from it. His chest wasn't well developed, but his very large nipples were the same dark color as his cock and balls.

"Seen enough?" he smiled.

"No," I said. "Stay there for a moment."

He didn't move. I imagined him as a proud mestizo in the Mexico of his ancestors. There was a warrior's pride about him, even in this humiliating stance. It made the sight much more interesting, much more delightful.

He was uncomfortable — something to add even more pleasure. He shifted from foot to foot and would alternately look away and then stare me in the eye, his face displaying a constantly moving series of emotions.

He moved to lower his shirt and I stopped him. "No, keep it up there, I want to see your tits." He complied.

The event was turning him on. His cock was getting harder. I sat there, silently, and watched as the curve increased its length and pitch. It was uncircumcised, its wrinkled hood added a beauty to it. The small bit that showed through the foreskin became even more erotic.

He, himself, looked at it at one point, as though he were studying a foreign part of his own body. When he'd done that, the erection quickly increased. Soon it was fully stiff and standing out at a proud right angle to his belly.

"Good," I said as I stood up. "You have a fine body, a very interesting cock. I'll keep it in mind if the occasion warrants a call to you. Now, I have to make some phone calls. I'll see you soon, Joseph."

There was a moment where he seemed lost by my statement. Then he hurriedly put his clothing back in order. I was leafing through the phone book, ignoring him.

"You're as kinky as those mirrors," he said finally. "Man, maybe you better not call me." He seemed a bit hurt.

"Whatever. I do want you and the others to come at ten o'clock tomorrow, though. I have to have the place in perfect order."

"Sure, sure." He was buckling his belt back again. "I don't have a problem with that." He went towards the door, hesitated, then looked back. "I didn't mean that, about you being too kinky. I can get into it."

"For the money?"

He shrugged his shoulders. "It's sex, man. Yeah, I'll do just about any sex for money."

"I'll remember that, Joseph."

A Duet

While I enjoyed the anachronism of my hotel as a place to sleep and entertain, I was not prepared to eat my meals in its restaurant. Instead, eager to get into the mood of San Francisco, I walked up the steep slope of Nob Hill and treated myself to a fine dinner at one of the first class hotels there. I had an early evening appointment and my body was still on East Coast time, so I ate well before the rush and let the handsome staff wait on me. They were just as happy to pay me extra attention in the off hours of their shift as not. The boredom of standing and waiting for the night's rush of diners was obviously not their favorite activity.

I ate slowly and enjoyed every moment of it. I found the waiters intriguing. They were — to my studied eye — quite obviously gay. While their service was perfect, they were also taking great liberties with me. They had identified a kindred spirit and thought their jokes and asides would be welcome. I fell into the joviality of it all and bantered with them, even if it did erode the perfection of the experience.

Still, they were delightful young men, happy to be living in San Francisco and happy to have someone at one of their tables who would and could talk to them.

I had a second cup of coffee to waste a little extra time. I knew that it would be only a fifteen minute cab ride to my destination and to be early would have completely spoiled the effect.

I sat and thought back over the answer to the ad that had produced the visit I was about to make. It was the most intriguing in its delicacy, the most appealing in what it could accomplish.

I was, after all, going to leave San Francisco after the party. Of course, I would walk away with new memories of Martin and I wouldn't be at all surprised if some of the other men involved in Sunday's occasion wouldn't also become a part of my life.

Aren't I still your boy?

The words — as familiar as they were — hit me when they moved through my mind. The accumulation of adventures brings with it an accretion of people. They become part of my life, they linger with me, the emotional bond becomes a part of me, just as it becomes a part of them, I'm sure of it.

The Christophers of the world can erect the most formidable barriers against it, but even theirs can be destroyed, ripped open, never to be put back into place. I dismissed the idea of taking on Christopher directly. No, I didn't want to invest the energy and there were too many other people involved who could be struck by the falling debris — his wife, the woman who had been lied to and emotionally cheated throughout his frolics, was certainly one of them. I wanted no responsibility for anything other than the overt sexual contract I had made with him. I would use him and he would be used as he wanted to be in his dreams. It would stay a masturbatory fantasy, but he would never enter into those secret parts of my self. He would not be like Martin.

But there were others... The two I was about to see tonight were after something so specific and so easily and well achieved by involving me in their lives that I could easily see myself performing a deed that one might call noble.

I smirked at that idea. The nobility of the sadist! What a fine ring that phrase had to it. But there was a slight bit of truth to it. They were in need. I held the means to meet that need. And I would leave, making the connection clean and clear and not presenting any tarrying complications. I would be a very good friend.

Finally, it was time to leave the restaurant. I paid my bill, leaving enough of a tip that the waiters would remember me fondly when I returned — and I knew I would return, for this was precisely the kind of grand hotel restaurant that Madame would enjoy. I went to catch a cab.

Phillip and Glen lived in a neighborhood that bordered the area South of Market. Their house was a Victorian, not really a very impressive building, but a solidly middle class two-story house that I was sure was worth quite a bit on the inflated real estate market. They had lived here for ten years, they'd told me. That meant, according to some quick mental calculations, that they had bought the house for a very small amount when it was little more than a shack and the area around it hardly the middle class enclave it had become.

The boys had done well. They'd described the hard work they'd put into the building, pioneers in those first waves of urban renewal. The structure looked sound, the paint on the outside was competent and attractive, the small yard was lovingly cared for.

I went to the front door and rang the bell. There was a sudden noise on the other side. I knew how very much tension can be built up by the expectation of a visit like this one. It had been arranged over a month before and the phone calls and the exchanged notes wouldn't have alleviated the worry and concern that they'd been feeling at all. In fact, each of our communications had produced an intensified reaction.

I'm not sure what it will mean to give up my role. The more I think about becoming a bottom, the more I worry what it will do to the way that Phillip looks at me. I worry about that. I worry about my need to be a bottom. It's not my only need, but it's a strong one. I still want to be who I've been to Phillip. I just want to be something else to someone else — at least once in a while...

Phillip answered the door. I recognized him from the photographs. His handsome skin was as impeccable as the pictures had made it look. He smiled; his tanned complexion seemed to dance with possibly natural highlights that actually seemed to convey a peach tone, and his teeth were as ideal as I had expected.

"Come in, please," he said, standing aside. As I walked by him I could sense the same kind of insecurity that Keith had shown — his hands seemed to move in midair for a split second. They didn't know if they were supposed to shake mine or stay out of the way. He bent his body slightly, perhaps in a half attempt to bow that was short-circuited by a realization that the melodrama of the action would be inappropriate.

I walked into the pleasant living area. Glen was waiting. He stood up and nodded. "Welcome."

I smiled, took a seat and accepted the offer of a glass of Scotch from Phillip. Glen sat back down on his own chair. He was obviously nervous. He was leaning forward with his elbows on his knees while his lover went about the host's duties in the other room. Glen's hands were clasped in front of him and his fingers were rubbing the back of each of them. I let him sit in the silence. It would have been a sham to make any comment to relax the young man, given what I had planned.

Glen was quite as attractive as his lover. They were both brown haired, but Glen's appeared darker, and his clean-shaven beard was obviously heavier. He was wearing an athletic shirt and I could see that his forearms were hirsute as well. I had seen a picture of him naked only from the waist up. From that I knew that his chest was as thickly covered as anyone would ever want it to be.

Phillip reappeared with my drink. He and Glen already had theirs, I saw. Too bad, it wasn't the best way to start. But their house had certain very distinct advantages over the hotel suite and I had decided that the use of what they proudly claimed was a well-equipped playroom made up for the inconvenience and distraction of allowing them the luxury of having the action taking place in their own space.

"Is the party still on?" Phillip asked in a conversational tone.

I was stunned for a second. "Of course," I blurted out, not understanding why he would ever have doubted it. But of course, I realized, there are so many who talk about their plans so well and so loudly and then never, ever come through. "Everything's in quite good shape. I assume you're still prepared."

Glen began to fidget, moving more in his seat and acting very uncomfortable, so much that I wondered if he was going to say no at this late date. But that wasn't what was on his mind.

"We are. God, are we!" He laughed then; it had a good solid tone to it and the smile that broke out on his face was full of good cheer and anticipation. He was finally looking at me. "We've been thinking about nothing else. We're a little scared, we told you that, especially me..."

Yes, they had told me that. This was a great experiment for them. A time of change in their lives and in their relationship. Not that its foundations were in doubt. I could tell that their protestations that they were committed to one another were true just by observing the look that passed between them now.

I sipped the Scotch and took in the sight. Phillip was not as large as Glen. He was probably five foot ten. He was well built; obviously he attended a gymnasium regularly.

He was wearing the same type of athletic shirt as his lover. His arms rippled with rope-like muscles and sinew as he moved to reach his drink. His chest was expansive and his waist was tight and compact. His nipples noticeably stuck out against the cloth. He had been, after all, the bottom in this relationship for quite a while and his nipples would have received a great deal of attention.

Glen's, on the other hand, weren't at all obvious through his shirt. His jeans were as well molded as Phillip's, the thigh muscles and the calves were obvious. I wondered how much experimentation he'd done before this one time. I thought now, as I had guessed earlier, that there hadn't been much. The authenticity in the way they had described their kinship and the length of time it had lasted didn't indicate that there would be a lot of lying or sneaking around between them.

I didn't speak. I let them sit with their thoughts. They had wanted this meeting to take place in a leather bar. That was so expected. I would have dressed in my uniform and they in theirs and the roles would have been set with dramatic effect. I could have been the prop for their psychodrama and that would have been so easy for them.

But I insisted the interview be in a social setting, not a sexual one. It is one of my most common conditions. They'd resisted, but then given up with the acknowledgement that they, themselves, were after more than the sexual. This encounter that I insisted upon would make them deal with their reality in a more concrete form. They acceded to my demands.

Now they were in their living room. The jeans, athletic shirts and worn black leather boots they both sported were obviously their most comfortable clothes. These were boys who lived in the neighborhood, for whom the stuff of the leather culture was simply taken for granted. Their clean outfits — and the lack of keys on Glen's left side — were accommodations for my pleasure. I understood that.

The downstairs was directly below us. It would have been

easy, also, if they had met me there, if we had gone right into the action — because the desire on all our parts was for action. The "interview" element in this visit was even less important than in the others.

These two men were making a trade with me.

Your party sounds like a wild time. It's not really what we would normally get into. I don't mean to be disrespectful, but it seemed to me that we could trade with you. If you'll help us out, we'll return the favor.

Glen looked at me and spoke first. "We heard . . . about you. We have a lot of friends in the leather world. They told us . . . you were the right person."

So that was the cause of their choice of me for this experiment. I hadn't investigated that before. It hadn't been of great concern to me. But, of course. I should have realized. The Network would be in effect. Many of the people who had recognized my advertisement would be talking.

People like Martin would have been building up the party for their own ego's sake: "I'm going to be a part of it." And people who knew me by reputation, the ones who could never quite believe that I had left this life and hadn't re-entered in so long, would be taking a gossip's pleasure in reporting my activities.

He's coming back. He was supposed to leave, but he's in San Francisco. An ad, a personal, a few men . . . that Martin, do you remember the sailor he used to have . . .

The Network is the one part of the sexual world that makes all of its enemies right. The other dangers and warnings they spout are stupid, meaningless. But there is a network of men — and women — who do communicate. That their subjects are willing adults and that their contracts are all highly consensual doesn't take away from the impact of their reality.

The Network is a conspiracy, a group of like-minded people who have drawn together and who spread word through a hidden chain of information — all the most modern forms — computer modems, telephones, video tapes. Who are the actors and where are they playing? The word gets out.

I hadn't paid attention to it in years. I had no real reason to. I simply knew that it was functioning. I hadn't stopped to think that, yes, my reappearance on the scene would be announced.

"What did these ... people tell you?"

"They weren't very coherent," Glen answered. "Some of them said, yes, he's the one. Others told us to watch out for you. But they couldn't — or wouldn't — explain why. If you'd been dangerous in any of the usual ways, I think I would have found out. I know a lot of people in the scene. But the warnings weren't that overt. They just said you were ... pretty heavy."

Pretty heavy! What an archaic term.

"And that didn't concern you? That I had that reputation?"

"No," Glen said. "Who we are and what we're doing needs someone who understands. I think you do." He finally sat up in his chair. "This is all very difficult, for me at least. I don't know, Phillip says it's all fine. But the changes in our selves and our relationship are pretty drastic. I take all this very seriously."

I could see that. Glen was speaking with as much veracity as he could muster. I saw the way he was studying me and I realized there was, indeed, danger here. There was ground being broken and the manner in which it was done by whom would not go unnoticed. My expectation that this was going to be a totally clean dynamic was being challenged.

That, certainly, didn't mean I was going to avoid what might happen. Hardly. I looked quickly back and forth between the two men and realized that this was certainly a remarkable find.

I had seen Phillip before in pornographic photographs and movies. When he had been much younger, before he met Glen, he'd acted in them. It was an expression of his masochism to let his body be viewed by as many people as possible. He claimed he'd never really needed the money, only desired the attention.

Now, like Glen, his looks had matured and the maturation was very much in his favor. He was a handsome man, not just a pretty boy. The training he'd given his muscles had filled him out, made him all the more appealing.

Glen had been the stronger of the two for almost all of their time together. He'd taken the raw material of Phillip ten years ago and insisted that it be disciplined, that it be structured and made to function in a responsible and planned manner. They were not, Glen had decided, going to fall into the traps of the gay world.

If it would take actual physical and sexual correction to make Phillip understand the seriousness of Glen's intent, all well and good. Glen would give it. They had entered into a well thought-out and articulated plan. They had saved the money for this house. In its basement they had constructed what they assured me was a complete stage set for their sexual needs.

Phillip had been led down the stairs as often as Glen thought he needed to be reminded and assured of his place in their lives together. Glen had gone and found older, more experienced men who explained to him the techniques, the methods and the finer points of the dominating sexuality that he wanted to deliver to his lover.

They had claimed that Glen became extremely proficient in his actions. The journeys to the cellar became more and more intense, the events more noteworthy, the ability he had to bring his lover to the peaks — and the depths — became more sophisticated.

It had worked for years. They had collected their leather and made the rounds of the parties, the bars, the weekend retreats and they had done it all just by themselves.

But they were young, their proclivities hardly set in concrete. Glen needed room to maneuver, he discovered. The performance he gave for Phillip's benefit had changed in his mind. It wasn't enough.

I suspect he simply relaxed. His insistence on taking over and disciplining Phillip's life was a simple way for him to insist on structure in his own. When it was achieved and those base necessities — a relationship he trusted, a home they owned together, the beginnings of a real career — were accomplished, then he found himself floundering, and other personal needs began to surface.

Glen was fatigued. His role had been all for Phillip. People who aren't experienced in the scene seldom understand how much the bottom, the slave, is usually the focal point of all the activity. It's not at all strange that Phillip had desired to display his body in endless numbers of pornographic photographs. Most masochists are gluttons for attention. At least, the ones who play-act at it are. There are those I admire and covet so much who are willing and able to resign themselves to another man's pleasure.

They are most often the ones who have experienced both roles. They, like Glen, have seen the flow of energy and understand that the bottom is being given a gift by his master. "Attention" is the right word. Think of the most devastating S&M event you can imagine and realize just who it is that is the focus for all the action.

It is a perversity of the real meaning of S&M that I seldom allow. It is worth it to me when the figure I'm being given to work on is truly worth the sexual energy involved. And, I realize, isn't that precisely what is going on between myself and Christopher?

But, that's not the point here. The point here, right in front of my eyes, is this pair. Phillip, a well-trained and experienced masochist, had lived his adult life under the service of his lover/master Glen. And Glen had allowed his own desires to build and build until they approached the breaking point.

Glen wanted to change his role. Phillip, it was obvious to everyone, couldn't and wouldn't provide the opportunity. And it would have been a violation of their contract, if either had entered a separate relationship with another man. They'd told me in letters that they'd thought about doing just that. This was San Francisco and it wasn't uncommon for people to have multiple relations. But there were the health concerns, of course. And there was the stickiness of the relationships.

Perhaps, they'd suggested, they could share the experience of serving at the party. They would come and attend as servants together. There was danger involved. That was the issue Glen had written to me separately about. What would happen to Phillip's vision of himself if he saw Glen in a servile role — and adoring it?

Of course it could work. Glen assured me that neither he nor Phillip wanted him to give up his role entirely. That was obviously going to have to be the dynamic between the two of them. But, if he could have his fantasies met, if he could enjoy the other side of the equation, if there were someone who wouldn't threaten their relationship . . . And I, of course, lived far away. I could be that person.

I understood even more of it now. It was finally getting into my mind that there might be no end to what would happen tonight. I thought of Martin and the way he carried the image of me through his life, the phantom master who could always be turned to when needed, if only for a masturbatory moment.

I studied Glen and wondered if I would be that person for him as well. On those occasions when they were having sex and the role of the master was too tiring, too demanding, when he needed the attention and the release from responsibility, would he be thinking of me from now on?

Another one, another one to carry in my mind and to hold in my dreams and fantasies. Such a handsome one, too.

"I'm ready to go downstairs. Are you?" I stood up before they could answer. The two of them wavered for the shortest period, then got up together, as though their movements had been synchronized.

Glen led us to a doorway in the hall that I assumed went to the basement. He stopped when his hand had taken hold of the handle and he turned to me. "We always make this our changing point," he explained in a way that let me know he meant that this was a major symbol in their lives. "From here on in, the language changes and the action begins immediately."

There *was* a boundary then.

Many men used the device, and it was a splendid one. Many men could not conceive of another who was a clerk during the day as someone who could, at a simple statement, change into the master. An effective means of dealing with it was to create a line — something as elementary as the entrance to the bedroom — past which the personalities changed. In the living room and the kitchen, the two men would be lovers, engaged in the mundane necessities of their existence. They could peel potatoes together, watch television and argue as peers. But once they moved over that line, then the other parts of their personalities were in force.

This stairway was that line for Glen and Phillip. Their theater was more intense and more dramatic than most. They would need to have a clear signal that the curtain was going up; the doorway provided it.

I wanted to show them that I understood. I turned to Glen and took him very gently into my arms. At first he didn't understand, he must have thought that I was trying to begin some of the action. But when it was apparent that I was only going to embrace him and kiss him, his body melted into it and he gracefully responded. I reached out a hand and brought Phillip in closer. His mouth was mine to kiss as well. The three of us stood there, our arms around all of our shoulders, and our faces pressing against each other. Glen sighed, delighted.

I went down the stairs first. When we had all reached the floor

I could see the startling difference in the attitudes of the pair of them. They had entered their sacred space and they were with the priest they had asked to reside over their services.

They moved slowly, but went about the tasks of creating the atmosphere for their rites. Candles were lighted in each of the four corners. They were all large and white, each sitting on one of a matched set of holders made of elaborately designed iron.

There were also the electric lights that we had turned on at the top of the stairs. They were all dim, the bulbs red-hued. But, with the candles, I could clearly see the details of the room.

In the very center was a table. The middle third of it was grounded on a stand, but I could see that the other parts of it were ingeniously constructed. They were hinged to the center piece. But their corners were attached to chains that were firmly attached to the floor and the ceiling. I understood immediately what effect they could have.

Another chain, even heavier, ran from the ceiling to a bolt in the floor. It stood like a sculpture beside the table. That, I knew, would prove to be interesting.

There was a shower stall, almost invisible behind a black rubber curtain that wouldn't have been noticed by an unsuspecting eye, and beside it a sink and a toilet. There was even a club refrigerator, probably stocked with beer and soda.

On one of the walls was an impressive display of implements. Whips, crops, leather straps, paddles, and canes were all in careful — even loving — place.

Another wall held just as extensive a collection of restraints, from simple handcuffs to antique looking shackles. There were lengths of rawhide and rope, masks made of leather and rubber, even a straitjacket for total immobilization.

I take all this very seriously.

Glen certainly did. I could imagine how long it had taken them to accumulate the tools for this room.

Phillip had moved to the other side of the room where there was a stereo. The rich sounds of orchestral music suddenly filled the space. He turned down the volume and then stood there, waiting.

Glen was by the table. His arms were behind his back, his head was slightly lowered, just as it had been upstairs.

These males, those who had been used to having the role of master, had strict and uncompromising expectations which they had developed over their years with masochists. They understood the perfection of stance, reaction, submissiveness and how very much it could be appreciated. They judged themselves very harshly, more willing and able to act for the master's pleasure than any other slave would be. Glen, with his pent-up frustations, knew he was suddenly in a room with someone who would understand and esteem the most subtle gestures. He would want to perform them exquisitely, and would do anything to avoid a lack of grace; he knew how disconcerting that could be.

The music lent another level to the sense of the religious and theatrical air of the room. The boys had worked hard at this place. Another wall was a gallery of photographs. Purposely ignoring them, wanting them to enjoy these moments of disquiet anticipation, I went over to study the photographs.

Most of them were clipped from magazines. Here were the pornographic ideals that the two of them must have shared. The images were expected: the muscled young men in leather, the hard-looking bikers, the harsh military officers. There were also their own photographs, obviously the most cherished self images they had. Glen in his leather, with his forbidding cap covering the top of his face, but his cock stiff and hard in the opening of his chaps. Phillip standing naked and collared, his arms bound behind him, his body marked with scarlet stripes after a particularly hard session. The two of them on a motorcycle in the country, both in leather, but both smiling.

"I want you both naked." I said the words without turning to watch them. They were in their temple and they understood that their clothing defiled it. Their skin would be more appropriate. I listened to the rustle as they both stripped quickly.

I turned and saw them both nude, awkwardly standing there, not quite sure what I had in mind for them next. There was a leather upholstered chair over by the fourth wall, a wall that was decorated only with a pair of large posters of drawings of men in leather. I went over and sat there.

Basement. What a strangely insufficient word to describe what this place must mean to the two of them. This was more intimate than their bedroom. It was the place where their secrets were shared and their risks were taken.

I sat in the chair and took in their bodies. Glen's body hair was as thick as I had expected, Phillip's as smooth. Their torsos were unflawed, the lines of their chests were perfectly matched fans, their thighs were thick and well defined. Both their cocks had begun to rise.

Glen was again standing with his hands behind his back. I could sense the tension in his body, expectation was taking hold of him. A small line of sweat was already making its way down the side of his stomach.

"You've never done this?" I asked.

"Never . . . *seriously*, sir," Glen responded. They had told me only a few things, just hints really, about the times when they had attempted having sex with a third party and one of the three of them had given up. That had been one of their problems. Finding just the right person to do the thing correctly.

"And it's something you want to share?"

"Yes, sir," Phillip answered this time.

Other men would have found the repetition of these questions and answers unnecessary — we had gone over them in the letters and phone calls. But these two understood, as I knew they would, the ritual benefits of what was going on. They were making their confession before their communion. The words must be said and the honor must be done with the priest in attendance.

"Come here, Glen," I motioned him with my hand. He came forward, his head still bent. When he was only inches in front of me, he stopped, leaving his still-filling cock directly in front of my face. I could see the wrinkles of his scrotal sac, the veins in his penis, the purple of the glans skin covering. There was an odor about him, of excitement, perhaps fear. There was dampness on his pubic hair from the emotions.

I ran my hand up and down his right thigh, testing the firmness of the flesh. It was perfect. I wonder sometimes if my indulgence in this special world of sexuality has only to do with my desire to so minutely examine male bodies. I adore having them so obviously and openly available to me. I can't imagine being one of those people who talk about wanting to commune with the whole person, wanting to have just the merger of souls. Of course, I know that and I honor that when it occurs, but this, male flesh, is a delight all of its own.

"Phillip." The other one moved over as soon as I spoke. He, too, was getting hard from the excitement of what was going to happen. I had them both in front of me. I reached out and in each hand cupped one of the sets of genitals. The soft feel of the feathery pubic hair of the testicles was perfect. I lifted up the two sets, as though weighing them. I applied no pressure, there was nothing to my touch that could possibly have created pain, but they both tensed, as though they expected it to come at any moment.

I let the two sacs fall back to their hanging position, and took hold of their two cocks. Both were circumcised, both well done. I pulled gently at the skin around the half-erect shafts and listened as the two men quickened their breath in response.

These were magnificent specimens. These were men I would be proud to own. I stood up in front of them, still holding onto their cocks. I moved them with those intimate handles to the center of the room. I let go and walked to the wall that held the restraints. Of course, my vassals stayed where I had left them.

I got what I needed and returned to them. I put the materials on the bench and calmly grabbed Glen's wrist. I quickly took up a pair of leather wrist restraints and attached them to his arms. He didn't resist at all, in fact he tried to be helpful and anticipate my movements. When the pair were securely fastened, I lifted his hands up in the air. I had taken small "D" clamps from the wall, and used them to lock the restaints to the heavy chain at a point far above his head.

I went back to the bench and took hold of a large metal device. At either end of a three-foot section of iron were ankle restraints. They were locked into place with a turn key. I applied them to Glen's legs, and the iron rod forced his legs apart, ensuring that he couldn't use his body movements at all to evade anything I would chose to do to him.

Glen was utterly defenseless now. I stood back and looked at him. His cock was even stiffer, though still not fully erect. His balls hung down in the air, unable to touch his thighs now that those were forced apart by the bondage. His eyes were wild. I wasn't sure if it was desire — the realization that his dream was coming true — or the sudden rush of emotion that arrives when a slave is finally aware of the physical paralysis that bondage can produce.

He moved against the restraints, as though testing them, and the heavy chain moved ever so slightly, just enough to produce a metallic sound of rustling. But that was all. It wasn't going to give. I wondered if he had been the one to choose the bolts that made it so securely fastened to the floor and ceiling. If he had, I thought he might have been damning his handiwork right now. There was no way he would escape this position.

I turned to Phillip. He was staring at the sight of his lover, the man who had led his own way for so long. When he realized I was looking at him, he seemed to freeze and then he actually moved a half step away from me. Whoever could do this to the man who had controlled him for ten years must seem a particularly frightening figure to him now. "Does he look good?" I asked.

"He looks wonderful, sir."

I ran a hand on the stretched area of Glen's chest, just on the side, away from the nipples, where the lines of his rib cage were forced against his skin. "Does he look any less a man this way?"

"Of course not, sir."

"Get a condom."

Phillip sprang into action. He went to a cabinet and brought back a foil-wrapped container. I unwrapped it. It wasn't one of the usual types. It was dyed black and, while it was latex, it would have the appearance of black rubber.

"Get him hard."

Phillip immediately fell to his knees and began to mouth at Glen's balls. His tongue, a tiny piece of pink, shot out and lapped at the hair-covered flesh. Glen began to struggle again, his hands tugged at the chain and his feet worked against the iron. While it was futile, it also produced a kaleidoscope of visual poses that sent a shiver of ecstasy through me. One after another of his muscles would come into sharp focus from the exertion, then relax back into the rest of him as he labored to respond to the stimulation of Phillip's tongue.

In a very short time he was stiffly erect. I pulled on Phillip's hair to remove him. The boy was showing his passion; he unthinkingly resisted at first, his tongue was still out even when I had him back on his haunches.

I took hold of Glen's cock and unraveled the condom onto it. The appearance of the black latex was wonderful, making it seem as though his erection was encased in a rubber trap.

I grabbed Phillip's hair again, harder this time. I twisted it in my fist until he opened his mouth in a silent scream. "Suck it." I threw his head forward so quickly and so hard that I was surprised he was able to manage getting the hard cock into his mouth. I crouched down beside him while he wildly went at his lover's cock.

"You love this, don't you? On your knees with that prick in your mouth? Naked, in front of your man, showing him how much you need his sex?"

Phillip didn't stop his abandoned sucking for an instant. He answered my questions with muffled sounds while he kept on going with such enthusiasm that spittle was flowing down the sides of his lips, running off over his chin.

I pulled him back again. He let out a sound like a wounded animal when he was removed from that object of desire. There was no doubt about how much he loved Glen's cock. His own was rock hard, standing up from his body at a sharp angle. I had watched — he hadn't had a chance to touch himself during any of this, his hands had been on Glen's hips. His excitement was just from the idea of being down there, worshipping his personal god.

"Get up."

I moved quickly and had wrist restraints on Phillip before he even understood what was happening. I lifted his arms up and attached them to the chain near the same point where Glen's wrists were locked. Then I put restraints on his ankles, clamping them to Glen's, forcing his legs just as far apart as his lover's.

Their faces were forced together as was most of the front surface of their bodies. I went to the wall and retrieved a long piece of rawhide. When I came back I found the two of them kissing each other, lovingly.

I took the rawhide and tied a section of it tightly around the base of Glen's balls, forcing the testicles to the furthest extreme of his sac and doing it so harshly that he couldn't help but moan in response to the pain. I took the rest and looped it just as tightly around Phillip's sac.

Their hips were forced to press even more closely to one another by the rawhide; I left no slack at all between their bodies. Their erections interfered with their desire to give some relief to the pressure on their balls, and the hard shafts of flesh squirmed between their bellies.

Now I brought back two sets of tit clamps. Both had moderate stress to them. These wouldn't be the easy stimulation that rubber tips could bring. The metal would bite into the flesh. I took one pair and put one of the clamps on Phillip's right nipple. He sucked in his breath when he felt the tight grip. The other end of the pair — they were joined together by a thin metal chain — went on Glen's own right nipple, crossing from one side of their chests to the other. I repeated the process with the other clamps, leaving an X of chain between them.

Their kiss before had been purely romantic eroticism. They had been reacting to the idea of their joint bondage. Now Phillip sought out Glen's mouth with a more desperate need, as the leather bindings of their balls and the biting pain of the nipple clamps became a shared ordeal that demanded their mutual support for it to be overcome.

I found a leather strap on the other wall. It was wider than a belt and had no buckle or metal studs to produce more pain than I wanted it to, certainly no damage. My twin captives were still kissing one another. But I wanted their attention. I stood behind Phillip and ran the leather across the wide muscular expanse of his back. He knew what it was — of course he did — and he knew it would be used. He drew back from Glen and stiffened, as though he could prepare and protect himself.

I moved in on them, wrapping my arms around their bodies so that my head was over the back of Phillip's shoulder and I looked directly at Glen. "I want you to know what happens when you beat him. I want you to feel him while it happens, and I want you to feel him knowing that you're going to receive the same thing."

Glen closed his eyes, almost in emotional pain. He was readying himself just as Phillip had been. I stood back and tested the leather on my palm. Its sting was perfect, more than enough to leave them with the sharp reality of a beating, but not so much that I was going to have to monitor my blows too severely. I stood back even further.

Phillip was clenching his ass to brace himself; the muscles were sharply defined and quivered exquisitely. I waited, enjoying the sight of the handsome flesh, pausing so that he wasn't too well set for the first blow.

Then I struck out at him. The leather was longer than a belt would have been. It allowed me to use it on the whole of both of his cheeks. It left one broad stripe of red across the white expanse of muscle. He reared up, no amount of preparation could have steeled him so well that he wouldn't scream at the shock of the whipping. When he moved, he jerked the rawhide holding his balls to Glen and the chains that joined their nipple, forcing his lover to experience the jolt of pain himself.

I kept the leather moving. It became like a brush, leaving a path of reds, pinks and purples on the two round halves of his ass, forcing him to jump first one way then the other. No matter how much he'd try to save himself and Glen from the added pain of the rawhide and the tit clamps, the whip would find a new spot to inflict a new torment.

I didn't just alternate the slams on his buttocks. I moved to more unexpected places. The legs were forced so far apart that there was easy access to the tender insides of his thighs. I had to soften the impact, of course, but even the slightest taps there were as effective as the most vicious assaults on the firmer and more defended buttocks.

The back of his calves were just as sensitive. The wide leather could find its mark there, and his feet were so tightly attached to Glen's that there was no way he could escape.

I moved up and down the lower half of his torso with the strap, hitting hard at one place, less so at another, and always doing it in ways that could never be anticipated.

I finally stopped. My own body was shaking from the work it had done and the leather hung from my hand. Phillip was sobbing, his chest wracked with contractions from the severity of the punishment. Glen was desperately trying to comfort him, raining kisses on forehead and neck and all over his face. I moved in close and put a hand on the hot surface of Phillip's ass. He jumped at the sudden contact, but immediately softened when he realized the intent of my touch.

I moved my palm over the skin, calming him, assuring him that there was no anger behind the assault, only appreciation of his offering. His chest slowed down, his sobs turned into weeping and he began to return Glen's kisses. When I moved in even closer, he turned his attention to me, moving his lips over my face hungrily.

The clamps had stayed attached to their nipples, the rawhide was still in place. I reached in and tested the chain between their chests and they both reared up from the added pressure. I kept calming Phillip; he'd persevered splendidly and deserved the recognition. But I wasn't being comforting to Glen when I looked at him. Instead I smiled — I probably was closer to smirking.

"It was your decision."

He hadn't indicated any desire to pull back from the choice of being there, in the bondage, waiting for his turn with the leather strap. But I was making sure he realized that the resolution to have him witness his lover's trial was purposeful — it was meant to make him more conscious of what he, himself, was going to suffer.

I moved to the other side of them. There was Glen's unblemished back waiting for me. His ass wasn't the pale and uncovered flesh that Phillip's had been. Instead there was a coating of fine dark hair all over it. His back was as muscled, if more streamlined. His legs were just as clearly strong. I ran my hand over the whole of him, from the neck down to his calves. He shook from that slight contact.

When I stood back, my strap ready again, his body was shaking. Phillip was staring. I knew that he'd never been able to see this before — not just Glen, his lover, being whipped, but any other man being beaten at such close and intimate range.

When I brought the strap back for the first time, Phillip's eyes opened broadly, as though in wonder, as they watched the leather travel to deliver a sound blow on Glen's buttocks.

Glen was clearly less used to the strap. He yelled out in pain from the beginning. But he wanted the experience, he needed the experience. I only let myself soften the assault slightly. I went through the entire scenario with him. I began at his ass, I moved down the insides of his legs, to his calves, back up again, alternating the blows, watching the richness of the colors as they came out, luxuriating in the control of his flesh's response.

His screams were loud all through it, his tears more copious, his useless attempts at escape more frenzied. His reactions kept tugging at the nipple chains and the rawhide bonds, bringing Phillip greater continued sensations.

Again, at about the same point, I stopped and walked up to Glen. I put my hand on his softened skin just as I had Phillip. I calmed him down, wiping the sweat from his brow and running my palm over his face with soothing motions. He thought it was done. He thought he had suffered all there would be.

"Phillip's been put in his place. He's come to understand the lash, to understand that he needs it and that it brings him a kind of peace. You, though, are only learning. You think you retain a sort of control. You're wrong. A slave has to be introduced to his pain to understand that it is an ever-present possibility. Phillip only needed to know that I could do it. That I had the strength to inflict the punishment. He didn't need to know how far it could go. You do, Glen. You need so much more than Phillip does."

The words forced a new and stronger flood of tears. There was no doubt in his mind that I was going even further than I had with his lover.

I took my place. I looked at the beautiful results of the first half of Glen's torment, the decorations that lined his buttocks and legs. Then I studied the unmarred surface of his back. I lifted the strap and brought it down on his shoulders.

Now he lifted up in immediate pain. The leather sang out as it sped through the air and repeatedly found its mark on his back. The bone is so much closer there and the flesh so much harder that the sounds were different than the music of leather on ass. They're more masculine in a way, stronger, deeper. They are evidence of infinitely greater physical hurt and psychological humiliation.

A man might have his ass beaten by another; a true slave has his back whipped.

When I was done, the marks were evenly spread over Glen. Only the dangerously vulnerable area around his midsection was unscarred. I stepped back in and again wrapped my arms around the two of them. Again, I listened as Glen's cries turned into whimperings. Phillip barely noticed me for a while, so intent was he on seeing what his lover was going through. There was a sense of awe about it. He would always remember — as I had planned — that Glen had suffered more and hadn't cracked.

Tears? Sobs? They mean nothing. They are inevitable and only a foolishly proud man would deny them when he's being put through all of this. But there was no denial, there was no vain attempt to escape, to have the punishment lessened. Glen had accepted it, just as Phillip had. The lovers were obviously proud of one another, each in his own way.

"Do you understand now what it means to have me here?"

"Yes, sir," they both said at once.

"Do you understand that it never ends with me?"

Phillip nodded, only Glen answered out loud, "We're yours, sir."

"For what?"

"For anything."

"I'm going to make you prove that."

I went about releasing them. The clamps let an extraordinarily painful surge of blood into their nipples and both cried out when the pressure was released. The removal of the rawhide was less dramatic. They were only glad to have some comfort back.

The intensity of the whipping had frightened off their erections. But as I went about the untying of the rope that had joined their testicles and rubbed at the sensitive areas, both their cocks were coming back to life. I rubbed their genitals and licked lightly at their tits to help them. By the time I had moved to their arms and had let them down, they were both semi-erect and smiling from the pleasure.

When their restraints were released from the chain, I went to their collection and brought back two leather collars. They understood immediately. Both of them fell to their knees. I put the collars on. I thought that Glen seemed to be actually proud of his. Then I attached a lead to each of them. Again, I didn't have to speak. They went to their hands and knees. I walked them around the table. There was no resistance.

I led them to the chair and left them for a quick moment while I went to the refrigerator. I came back with bottles of beer and a glass bowl I had found. I opened two of the bottles, keeping one for myself and then pouring the other into the bowl.

The music was still going. While the strains of a baroque symphony filled the room, my two young men lapped at the beer in the bowl, thirsty from what had happened, knowing there was more to come. When they'd finished it they used their tongues to wash each other's face clean of the beverage that they'd spilt in their hurry. Then they looked up at me, anxious, smiling and waiting. They were watching my crotch, staring at the length of my cock, knowing they were going to get that reward as well.

I looked over at a clock. It was only ten. I didn't leave the basement until six in the morning. I knew that there were to be two extraordinarily well-trained young men to serve at my party.

Preparations

Joseph arrived with his crew the next afternoon. I'd barely slept three hours, but was refreshed, still exhilarated from my evening with Glen and Phillip. I showered and dressed while they began in the front room. Then I left them and went out to lunch.

A cab took me to Fisherman's Wharf where I indulged in watching the tourists make fools of themselves while I ate a decent meal in one of the many restaurants there. The crowd of middle Americans pressed too hard for me, though, and I left right after I ate.

I walked for miles, it seemed, up and down the hills, watching the changing view of the Bay and fog as it kept trying to spill over the Twin Peaks in the distance — a sight I could catch at the top of each hill.

I eventually went to the Castro and sat in a bar with an open facade, a wall on the street that rolled up and left me with a clear vista of the march of gay men up and down the street.

This had long been one of my favorite neighborhoods, though not for any social or political reason. In fact, it offends my Eastern sensibilities in some ways. More and more it seems to be too much like the other tourist areas of the city. But the sheer mass of gay men in their tight jeans, all of them ready to strip off their shirts at the slightest hint of warm sunlight, is a hedonistic delight that I can't compare to many other urban landscapes.

I eventually made my way back to the hotel. The work had been done and the suite was immaculate, incomparable to the shape it had been in. The wood surfaces had been scrubbed, the drapes and rugs vacuumed, the windows polished. All of the dust was gone. Joseph had obviously raided more than the cleaning stores of the hotel. One table which had been scarred was replaced by a newer one without any imperfections. The sheets on my bed, barely adequate, had been replaced with obviously new ones.

I was surprised that Joseph and another of the crew were still there. They walked me through an inspection tour. There was no doubt that they'd done their work well and I paid the agreed sum and added a large tip. When Joseph didn't leave, I understood that there was another agenda here.

His friend was Robert. He was about twenty, blond, and appeared to be nicely built. I gathered from little pieces of conversation that he was new to San Francisco. He'd gotten a job here at the hotel as a houseman, doing the heavy cleaning — vacuuming the corridor rugs and moving furniture. He stood off to the side, his hands in his pocket, while Joseph did the talking.

"You know, that kinky stuff you like, what we did? I told him about it," he shook his head towards Robert. "He's up for it too. You know, for a little money?"

Joseph smiled and tried to speak in a mano a mano tone of voice. "He's pretty hot. I've fixed him up with some of the guys who stay here. Real hot. He'll do anything, man, he really needs the money."

Robert showed none of the enthusiasm for sex that Joseph had. With the first youth, one had a sense that it was a game to get paid for it. It was some kind of con that he was running. He left the distinct impression that he would have fallen into it by himself and given it away if he was sure that there was no possibility of monetary reward.

Robert didn't display any of that. He appeared sullen. Those hands were dug so far into his pockets and his shoulders were so slumped up with anger that there was only the sense that this was some last-ditch effort he was making.

"Are you that broke?" I asked him. He didn't move, didn't relax at all. He only shrugged. I turned back to Joseph, "And what's your cut?"

"Finder's fee," he smiled. "I gotta get something for putting you in touch with him. He's almost cherry, man. Never done it with a guy until a couple of months ago. You must like that. You don't find many males who are almost virgins in San Francisco these days, that's for sure. Here's your big chance."

Joseph was overdoing his salesman's rap. I wasn't at all pleased with the crudeness of the conversation. "I'm not interested, Joseph. Forget it." I spoke to Robert then. "You're very handsome. I don't mean to insult you, but I'm tired now. Thanks for all the work on the rooms. I really appreciate the good job you've done."

They left, sulky and dissatisfied. I decided to go back to bed to catch up on the sleep I'd lost.

I barely heard the knocks through the dreams I was having. I simply integrated the sound into whatever it was that occupied my sleeping thoughts. But they were so insistent that I had no choice but to abandon my slumber's adventures and wake up. I grabbed a robe and went to the door. It was Robert. He was in the same petulant mood as earlier.

"What is it?"

"I . . . um . . . really am up for it, what Joseph was saying? I mean, if you're looking for someone, I'll do it and cheaper than he said I would."

"Joseph never mentioned an actual sum."

"Well, he told me I'd get twenty if you fucked me. I really could use the money, you know."

"Come in." I stood aside and pointed his way to the sitting room. I turned on some lights before I sat down; it was well into the evening now. "What do you need this money for?"

"I want to go home." He was looking straight down to the floor. "I want to get out of this place. I just need a bus ticket. I got paid today, if I can get some more together, I'll make it."

"Where is home?"

"Pennsylvania, near Pittsburgh."

"How did you get here?"

"With this guy, a guy I knew at home. We were going to live together and everything. It was too hard back there, but we thought it would work here. I followed him, I guess. He's gone now. Found some big stud bartender and moved out on me."

He spoke all this without any passion, as though he deserved the pain and hurt that he was describing. There was no indication that he was fighting off any of the emotions. He was a passive sponge for the waves of bad luck. More, I realized he probably attracted them.

"Where do you live now?"

"Not far, over near Polk. I still have the room we got together, a furnished place."

"Is there anything there that you need? Anything to get you back to Pennsylvania?"

"No."

Of course there wouldn't be. He hadn't any reason to accumulate memories of the city.

"I'm not interested in you sexually, I was honest when I said that."

Robert stood immediately. He shoved his hands back into his pockets and started to walk to the door.

"Stop." He froze in place, but didn't turn to look at me. "I don't want you to drown in California, though. Are you going to do anything with yourself if you go back to Pennsylvania?"

"I want to go back to school. I never finished high school. That's why I took this lousy job, I couldn't get any other kind. And I'm no good at hustling. I'm just no good at a lot of things."

"It's probably a waste of time and money, but I'll send you back home. At least you won't have the luxury of blaming other people for your bad luck from now on. You're going to have to live up to the fact that someone did you a good turn."

Now he swiveled around and look at me with disbelief. I went into the bedroom and quickly got dressed. "Let's go. I'm not giving you cash you can squander. But I'll buy your ticket."

An hour later I stood in the Greyhound station and watched the bus pull out. It would take him a few days to get to Pittsburgh and I could only hope that the little money I gave him was spent well enough that he could eat.

What a waste. I walked back up to Market Street and was even more aware of the many poorly dressed, ill-fed people who were lingering hungrily around the bus terminal neighborhood. We throw away our children, starve them nearly to death, then wonder why they turn to petty crime.

The circle of poverty and ignorance is vicious, never ending, the one true sadistic fact of American society. I could never have taken a boy like Robert who would only offer himself out of desperate need and unhappiness. My wrestler fantasy demanded a freedom of choice. My reality said that I could pay Joseph for his humiliation because he was an entrepreneur, not a victim. The Roberts of the world aren't a challenge for a man, they are the targets of vultures.

Collections of punks stood on street corners, probably to victimize the other poor people. They would rob the old ladies on social security, beat the women on welfare, rape the young men living on disability.

They disgusted me. There might be a nobility to the criminals in the worlds of Andre Gide and Jean Genet, and that was a nobility that attracted me. I feel a kinship with it. But these throwaway adolescents who feed on the walking wounded aren't that. They're volatile energy ready to land on anything that shows weakness. Such a waste of decent manhood.

I spied one of a group — handsome, well-muscled, black-haired and hard-looking with a cigarette dangling from the edge of his lips. We glared at one another. He began to follow me. I hoped he wasn't going to be foolish enough to try to start anything with me, certainly not in the bright lights of Market Street.

"Hey, mister, want a smoke?" He was holding out a package of Marlboros. I stopped and wondered what he was up to. Out of perverse interest I stood long enough for him to catch up with me. I took one of his cigarettes and let him hold a match out.

"You interested? Huh?"

"Interested in what?"

"Me," he laughed, as though my question had been silly. "What do you think? I got a big one and I know how to use it."

It was a warm summer night and he was only wearing an undershirt. I could see a whole collection of crudely done tattoos on both his arms, the type of amateur effort usually done in prisons and juvenile detention homes.

"No. Thanks any way. I'm not up to it."

I started to walk away, but he grabbed one of my arms. "Come on, man. I can throw you a wicked fuck. You'll like it."

This was, unquestionably, a perfect specimen of rough trade. I knew many men — many, many men — who would have adored it. They would have wallowed on their knees in front of him and eaten in his cock — big or small — and dreamed their fantasies of danger and real men, whatever that means.

"No." I repeated myself and took away my hand.

"Faggot," he snarled when he realized I wasn't going to play his game. I kept on going.

I went slowly up Market and then towards Union Square. The crowds only got larger, the waste of human life more obvious. I was burning with rage. Here was all the evidence of the unwillingness of society to deal with and care for its members.

Give them to me, I thought. I quickly envisioned myself at home; perhaps I'd need to buy a few more acres of land. I'd take the violent and anarchistic young males that terrorized the city streets, proving their "manhood" by being stupidly criminal. I'd turn my acres into a farm. They'd work their asses off. Naked in the summer, they'd pull the plows, their butts red from the strap. They'd sleep in dormitories, they'd eat wholesome food. They'd go to school in the morning — and no ridiculous social worker crap about modern theories.

They'd learn how to read and write and they'd study hard. No humanistic understanding about missing homework, only the well applied strap. No worry about schedule, a series of overseers would make sure they were on time. No time for wasted analysis on why they'd gone wrong; they'd be too tired from work and study to lose sleep over the past and would only want to graduate to a future.

They wouldn't try to fool themselves about manhood being something you got because someone weaker was frightened of you. When they learned to take it up the ass and to receive honor by having an adult choose them for a sex partner they'd have something much more real to measure themselves against. The failing of the whole social services system could be overcome by a confederation of sadists. I thought of Madame taking in a street boy, her cane in hand, his face being scrubbed — hard — and his nails cleaned daily. After a year of it he'd walk away with his education, all right, and a skill. He'd be able to be one of best waiters in the city, impeccably serving food in the finest restaurants. He'd have learned it quickly, and that swinging cane of hers would have embedded each lesson in his mind more efficiently than a horde of Berkeley graduates who would spend their time empathizing with him.

You think I'm wrong? Then realize this: The only effective therapy institution in the United States today, when it comes to dealing with young male criminals, is the Marine Corps. Talk to them, ask the young recruits why they're there. They'll tell you, as they've told me, that they needed the discipline. They were wild, dangerous, they saw their friends going to prison, caught at exactly the same activities that they were committing nightly. What was their option?

They self-medicated with a visit to the recruiting station and handed themselves over to the beast of a Drill Instructor who had them crawling on hands and knees and polishing boots and understanding that they needed it all within twenty-four hours.

My farm could do wonders for this scum that lined the city streets here and every other city in America. These wasted fools think they need "turf" to know where they belong in the world. I'd give them a sense of place with an engraved collar to remind them where it was. They whine about being denied opportunities that would make school worthwhile. I'd give them the motivation they needed to learn — a strap of leather they'd kiss every morning when they woke up, just to remind them that it was there. They cry that no one understands or cares for them. I'd show them the ultimate caring of S&M — the total observance of every minute detail of their minds and body by another being.

Reform school? *Hah!*

The Beginning

Madame arrived the next day. She called early in the afternoon and we agreed to go to the convention floor with one another. As always, she insisted on staying in one of the most elegant hotels in the city. I went there and had to go through phalanxes of uniformed personnel to get to the elevator.

She answered my knock immediately. "How wonderful," she said sleepily, then offered me her cheek to kiss. "I've had coffee and croissants brought up." She vaguely floated a hand towards the set table.

The red hair she's so vain about was piled on top of her head in a Victorian manner. A tight silk collar was wrapped around her throat and held in place by a small, elegant cameo. Her clothing, while chic and from the finest stores in New York and Paris, was all reminiscent of decades old fashion with puffed sleeves and much longer skirts than one would ever see on the usual businesswomen on the streets.

We talked about little. She was, underneath her facade of relaxation, desperate for me to discuss the party. I wouldn't give her the satisfaction of opening up the topic; I silently insisted that she ask me.

Finally she gave in, "Well, have your plans progressed at all?" One eyebrow arched in a schoolmarm mimic she so often affects. "Or am I simply taking you to your favorite restaurant again?" It was a challenge that she underlined by taking a particularly sharp bite out of a chocolate bun.

"Everything is progressing perfectly well," I defended myself.

"You'll be pleased."

Pleased? She was going to be in heat with what I had planned. She made those little gestures she does so well to let me know we'd see about that.

"Is Adrienne coming to the convention today?" she asked, moving the conversation away from the dangerous area where we both might feel like competing.

"No. I spoke to her yesterday. She can't simply walk through it any more. She'd be mobbed and can't deal with the idea of actually having the guards one of her publishers offered her."

"*Guards!*" Madame was suddenly transported into an obvious state of excitement.

"Yes, evidently they do it all the time for the big authors — Stephen King, Jackie Collins."

"In uniforms?" There was a new chocolate croissant stuck in mid-air as Madame entered a dreamy state.

"I suppose." I should have been prepared for all this. Of course it would get to her, the idea of a woman moving through adoring crowds and having to have to be protected by her staff of strong hired men.

"Why isn't she doing it?" Now Madame was back down to earth. She was openly incredulous that anyone would pass up the splendid opportunity.

"It's not her style. Adrienne isn't like us, you know that. We live our private theaters; her life isn't so crowded with the details we insist on. She doesn't demand that the world conform to her fiction the way we do. She doesn't cross the lines between fantasy and reality so often and so easily.

"Not that she wouldn't like to do it, but it's not her life. She's married to her first husband. She's a mother. A distinguished novelist who cares about her literary reputation. She doesn't care about creating her life as we do; she's more intrigued with her books. Her words live for her so incredibly well that she doesn't need the actions to go with them as emphatically as we do."

"But the party? She wants this party as badly as I want it."

"She wants it because she trusts that I can do it as well as she could have written it. She wants to see her words. These are her fantasies. But they're all translated by someone else. They take on a new look and a different feel. It's amazing to witness it.

"Besides, she cares about the details so very much. You know how bitterly anxious she is that we discovered things in her books that weren't possible. Here is an opportunity for her to attend a ... laboratory. She can witness the actual sight and feel and smell of it all."

"I don't believe you'll pull it off." There, she'd said what she'd been thinking. "I just can't believe that we'll sit in a San Francisco hotel suite with Adrienne and Phil and that it will all happen."

"Will you be disappointed if I do?"

"Hardly. I'll be astonished and I promise I'll respect you even more than I do now." With that she stood up and walked over to place a kiss on the top of my head. "We should go to the convention now."

* * *

The floor of the convention center was packed with milling crowds. The meeting is the one large professional event of publishing. I stood on the escalator as it descended to the lower level and gazed at the incredibly long lines of booths.

Madame was beside me, doing her own reconnaissance. "Amazing, isn't it. Whenever I see this I cease to wonder about how people manage to be published and instead am amazed that anything ever goes unpublished."

We got to the main floor and began to stroll up and down the aisles. Every publisher was represented. There is a cartoon that was once given out by a major house. A character goes up to a clerk and asks for a book. What kind, he's asked. Cookbooks, diet books, cartoon books? No, the character says, I want a novel. The clerk is bored. That would be under antiques, he says.

So it seems here. There are extravagant exhibits for books on every possible inconsequential subject that one could imagine. There are displays for supposed novels on Hollywood, the Riviera, and other romantic locales. There are ... There's a lot, and little of it is literature.

Especially not the literature that Madame and I create. But that doesn't keep us from being recognized by many of the editors whose displays we pass. There are some squeamish ones who've had sex with one or the other of us and there are those who we enjoy socially. But more of them are business acquaintances.

Whatever else we are, Madame and I are known on this floor.

Not for those selves that we've created, the sexual beings who constantly push against the lines between reality and fantasy, but because of the mundane earthiness of our lives. She is the editor of one of those magazines that everyone claims never to read, but which sells hundreds of thousands of copies a month to loyal readers. Those readers make her powerful in the eyes of even the most ostentatiously pretentious literary editors. There is no strength more valued on this convention floor than the ability to sell books.

I am ... worthwhile. I can take the boring subjects that these people want to have in book form and create enough words with enough ability to justify a front and back cover. I am not so important that I am to be courted, I understand that. But I'm treated well. No one knows just when he or she might not need me.

We lingered at various places. Madame tried vainly to be excited by the image of a bodybuilder who was autographing books that featured photographs of his grotesquely over developed torso. But she couldn't manage to make him a pornographic ideal. "He hardly has any meat at all," she said, dismissing him with that judgment of the small pouch that showed in his tight pants.

We moved along, stopping in one place to chat with one of Adrienne's editors. He was charming, shockingly handsome with his good looks, dressed in a three-piece suit. Of all the people we talked to, he was the one who would need us the least. His books were too refined to ever need coverage in Madame's sex magazine and little of my writing would ever be graced with the imprint of his house.

Perhaps that's why he was able to be so gracious, there was no need for anything but genteel discussion, and he was awfully good at that. He charmed Madame with flattering comments on her dress and spoke sternly to me about the elusive work that he and I had spent too many lunches dreaming about — the "serious" book he insisted I had in me.

When we walked away from him, I felt chastised by his questions. Madame felt the conversation gave her a free rein to jump on me. "There you have that great editor waiting for your masterpiece and you flitter away your time with silly boys and your impossible life in the country. You should be ashamed of yourself."

"Would you want me to stop writing about sex?" I teased her.

"Never!" There was actually a little bit of hurt in her voice. The idea that I'd end my sexual fiction appalled her, as I knew it would.

"He will never publish it." I said.

"But he published Adrienne's!"

"Adrienne is a name, a proven talent, one of the great living novelists. Adrienne can be forgiven for writing about sex. A gay man who does it and doesn't accompany it with something they decide is literature doesn't find his works in hard cover with that imprint."

"They should. They should all publish you."

I had a quick fantasy of the miles of displays here at the convention, all of them with huge reproductions of my book covers with their graphic depictions of men in bondage and leather. I decided I should change the topic.

"Have I ever told you how Ken expects it would be to have him edit?"

"That handsome young editor? Why he would certainly be the pinnacle of professionalism." Madame insisted.

"Ken agrees, but thinks there'd be a different form of professionalism involved. He once submitted a manuscript to that man and spent two weeks in agony, hoping it would be rejected."

"He wanted it to be rejected?"

"Ken couldn't imagine ever saying the word 'No' to anyone who was that physically attractive. He spun out the details of how it would be to work with him.

"He envisioned the editor wearing nothing but a sparkling clean jock strap. Don't ask me why the jock had to be clean..."

"Of course it would have to be on that man!"

"Then you agree with Ken. The editor would be seated wearing that jock and a white athletic t-shirt. He'd have a leg swung over the arm of a chair, the full pouch visible in every detail to Ken who would be sitting naked on the floor.

"Every time there was a minor flaw in the manuscript, the editor would bash him one, forcing him to do something horribly humiliating as punishment. But, when he found Ken had produced a particularly well-turned phrase or created an especially powerful image, he would reward him with a pat on the head or an affectionate tousle of the hair."

Madame stopped short in the aisle and put a hand on her breast. "S&M editing," she whispered. "It's too perfect."

"He's too perfect," I answered and led her further away from the booth.

We found one of Phil's publishers later and looked over a large pile of his books. The publisher was pleasant, but acted as though he didn't know quite what to do with us. Madame produces that reaction in people. They've heard all the stories about her and her magazine's reputation is no less than notorious. They expect, no doubt, that she should be cheap, slutty. They seldom are prepared for her well-groomed and well-attired presence and certainly are shocked by her highly cultivated voice.

I have to admit that I must create a similar problem for them. I, in their minds, should be clothed in full leather and probably should have a scarred face and a deep, gravely voice. I am often told that I should be even older than I am, probably alcoholic with a pot belly and vile cigars sticking from my mouth. That is the most popular vision of a pornographer. In fact, I look my Yankee heritage and almost all of my clothes are from L.L. Bean.

With my life and my writing, I feel little need for additional costuming.

"Where is the dear old man?" Madame asked after Phil.

The publisher's eyes raised in surprise. I doubt that many people have ever called Phil that, dear old man. "He's going to be here to sign his books on Saturday. I don't really expect him before then."

"Do we get him earlier?" she asked me.

"You can call and see if it's possible for the two of you to meet. I don't want to see him before Sunday. Nor Adrienne. I want the party to be the whole thing."

"Really," she replied with a slight humor in her voice, "you're going to pass up one of your marathon conversations with Adrienne? No afternoon with you and a bottle of Scotch and her with her endless cups of coffee?"

"Monday," I answered, a little embarrassed to be caught in such an obvious manner. "We've set aside Monday for one another."

"I'm not surprised." She was leafing through another book. "Will you and I dine tonight?"

"I have business tonight, a publisher. Tomorrow?"

"Fine. That place you like. I'll call Phil later today and see if I can't get him to come across the Bay for me."

"You're only doing it to see if he thinks you're important enough for such an effort. It's selfish, he's an old man. Why don't you go to him?"

"I think a dinner at the Mark Hopkins is worth anyone making a little sacrifice, no matter how old."

"Go ahead, he'll probably agree. Though you should be ashamed of yourself."

"I always am," she answered.

Martin

Martin arrived on Friday night.

As soon as he walked into the suite, we began to kiss. Our hands roamed over one another in some undisciplined fashion, as though the need to assure ourselves that we were both there was more important than anything else. We broke off after a while, laughed, then sat down on a couch together.

We quickly caught up on more news than we had been able to on the phone. I listened to some of his stories, he heard some of my own. There was a little game playing, a few harsh words from me just to remind him of our roles, some jockeying for position on his part, but none of it undermined the essential emotion, the happiness to be together and the relief as well.

I took him to dinner at a French restaurant on one of the avenues south of Market. The place was wonderful, and it was a kind of food that he usually would enjoy, but he was unhappy over something, I could tell.

I got him to talk: "It's nothing wrong with this. I'm just unhappy about what used to be and isn't any more. Don't you remember what a special place this neighborhood was? The way it used to be to come down here? And now it's French restaurants and fancy nightclubs, leather bars turned into straight discos and warehouses renovated into loft condominiums..." His voice trailed off in disgust.

I didn't argue with him. So much had changed, of course it had. Not just in the types of businesses that were here and the erosion of the uniqueness of being first gay and then also a man in leather, but there was the cloud of decaying death here as well.

That I couldn't change. I could find a new bar, I could try a new club, I could find a new outlaw dress that hasn't made it into the pages of *Interview* magazine, but I can't deport a virus...

We dropped the subject. We both knew that we had each said too much about it at other times and there was nothing to be gained by going through it all again. The reality was part of our lives and we knew it.

The topics went on to my party and my plans. I described the men to him. He demanded details. I described Keith, Christopher, Glen and Phillip to him. There were still others.

"Do I get to talk to them with you?"

"No. This is my creation. I want to do the interviewing myself. Besides, you have work to do."

"More interviews?"

"Hardly. You're going shopping."

He was furious; the blood came up to his face and I thought he'd slam the table with his fist. "What the hell do you mean, *shopping*? I came all the way from Los Angeles..."

"To go shopping. There has to be food ordered, arrangements to have it delivered, a few other things."

"While you're out fucking?"

"Are you jealous?" I was laughing at him, making him only more angry.

"You know I'm not. That's not part of the deal. I just don't see why I get to do that while you're off doing the rest."

"You get to do necessary tasks because I paid your air fare and you're staying in my hotel room. You're going to have more than enough enjoyment out of all this on Sunday. And tonight."

"And tonight?" That seemed to end the dispute immediately. "All right. I know I said I'd do the work for you. I will. What do you need"

We finished dinner talking about the small details, the places each of us remembered where certain items could be gotten. Over coffee he seemed to begin to relish the idea of what was to come. He began to tease me with more coy little remarks. I was playing with him. He didn't realize that his fun tonight wasn't going to be with me.

"You don't understand," I finally said. "You have work to do tonight, but it's work that you're going to enjoy."

"Without you?"

"Yes. The one I told you about, the big bodybuilder, Christopher, he needs some special treatment. A visit to his hotel room by you would certainly give him that."

"You don't want me?" It almost wasn't a question. It carried with it a real sense of hurt. I felt sorry I'd even played with him a little bit.

Aren't I still your boy?

"Later, and I'll want you as badly as you expect I will. But there's more I have to do. This must be perfect, Martin. It must be something that the rest of them all remember. I have two more men to interview and decide just what to do with. And it is important that this Christopher gets what he needs. I would have thought you'd like to be able to try out all of your new-found master talents."

"And you'll have to come up with designs for Sunday as well."

"All right, then just explain what it is that I have to do with this man. If you insist that I take on some well-built hunk of a bodybuilder, I suppose I'll simply have to give in to it. You always have been such a demanding master." Back in the hotel room we changed clothes. I put on more casual attire. It was carefully chosen to fit my purposes later on in the evening. I knew from the letters I'd received from Carl that my appearance needed a certain flair to it. I wouldn't completely respond to his desires, but there was no need to fight them totally, at least not in the beginning.

I finished first. Martin had been talking excitedly. The image I painted of Christopher was turning him on. He loved the idea of the man who wanted to be used but who didn't want anything but his body to be involved. I sat on the bed and watched him changing.

It was so familiar, every line of it was exactly as I'd remembered it. The torso was hairless except for blond bursts under his arms and over his crotch. The smooth expanse was just as muscled as I had expected his working out to have created. But he was so tall that the impact of the muscles wasn't as strong as it would have been on another man or on one as over-developed as Christopher. One had to study the thickness of Martin's thighs to see how large they'd become. The arms were well trained, to be sure, but on a man over six feet tall they just didn't appear to be as perfect as they would have on a shorter person.

But, then, there was his ass. He bent over to take off his briefs. I was sitting — without any plan — in the perfect position to see the freed buttocks as he angled his torso. They were perfect. They were large, like the rest of him, and there wasn't a mark on them. The pale skin simply bowed out, emphasized by his posture. He stood, reached into his bag and brought out a jock strap. He curled his body again. Now, when he stood up, the white ass was framed by an even whiter outline of the elastic straps.

He pulled on black leather pants over the jock. He'd decided to wear only a leather vest. It was still warm out. We both knew perfectly well that San Francisco weather wasn't at all predictable; it could easily become chilly later on. But Martin was going on an assignment in leather and to do less than adorn himself perfectly would have perverted his art. This thinking — foolish though it might be in some ways — is only one of the reasons I love him so.

His boots came next. Then a leather cap. He put on reflector sunglasses, their mirrors replacing his eyes. As soon as he was finished, his smile disappeared. He turned to me, his thumbs hooked in his belt, his stomach sucked in, his chest expanded to its full width. He posed, perfectly, just for me.

I stood up and took him in my arms. He wouldn't relax into my embrace. His transformation had taken place. But I wasn't going to allow this. "Do I have to beat you?"

Then, slowly, his arms lifted up and surrounded my shoulders and we kissed.

We took the elevator down to the lobby. As we walked through it, all eyes seemed to be glued on Martin's remarkable visage. He knew it, his steps were stronger, his stride longer. Joseph was there, just getting off duty I assumed — he wasn't wearing his uniform. He openly gaped at the two of us as we walked across the floor to the front door of the hotel.

I smiled and waved at him. Perhaps he would end up at my party after all.

A Military Presence

I wasn't at all surprised by Carl's attitude or his dress. "Sir." That was all of the greeting I got. But I'd expected that. He was wearing a pair of fatigue pants; from all indications they were authentic and probably from his own days in the service. He had on an olive-drab athletic shirt and a pair of brightly shined boots, again, probably authentic. The dark green colors set off the richly mahogany skin. His hair was close-cropped, but not so much that I couldn't see the tight natural curls of his African heritage. He was a proud and handsome man; some real indications of his warrior background were evident.

I wondered about that, as I had before. Is there something about some men that is bred into them by their ancestors — something that they spend their lives trying to discover in this modern, vanilla world? How do those men, who are by nature warriors, find their place in the world if the tight structures of modern society don't provide them?

Even his studio apartment took on the convincing air of a barracks. His bed was a simple metal cot. The wool blanket was stretched tautly and the sheet top evenly displayed over its top. There were only two chairs in the small apartment, both of them canvas director's chairs. Between them was a small, polished table with only about a one-foot square surface. The floor was as polished as his boots, the wax applied in many even coats. Not a thing was out of place. Even the kitchen was in military order.

The walls were either freshly painted or else laboriously

washed. On them were only a very few decorations. I walked over to take a look. There were a few inexpensively framed photographs of a military camp. The males in the photographs were all young, surely only teenagers. They were smiling boyishly into the camera. I could make out Carl in all of them.

I turned away and found him standing in perfect parade rest in the center of the room. His eyes were staring into space directly ahead. I moved toward him. He didn't move or flinch. I stood inches away. I listened to his breathing as it slowly but surely began to pick up speed. I began to study the rest of his body, letting my eyes travel downward.

When I got to his crotch I found a very expected bulge. Just having a man walk in here and allowing him the moment of his military presentation was turning him on.

"Have you read your orders?"
"Of course, *sir!*" He barked the last word.
"And you've followed them?"
"Of course, *sir!*"
"Have you any questions?"
"No, *sir!*"
"Proceed."
"Yes, *sir!*"

His face was flushed red. I took one of the folding chairs and waited. He swiveled so he was facing me. With great care — meticulous care — he began to mechanically remove each piece of his clothing. He folded the athletic shirt carefully and placed it neatly on the floor by his bed. Somehow he managed to retain his military posture while unlacing and removing his boots and pulling off his socks. The boots were stood side by side under the cot with the socks carefully placed inside them. Then came his pants. He couldn't have been more careful with their crease if they had been formal trousers. Standing now with only a cloth Army cap and his briefs on, he seemed to hesitate — only very briefly — but then took off the hat. Then — again, with the slightest hesitation, just enough to make this sexually fascinating — he pulled down his briefs.

Naked, he resumed his posture. The military truly has such a sexual component to it. Here was this man, standing just the way his drill instructors had taught him, and the result, once the offending clothes were taken off, couldn't have been better designed by a pornographic artist.

His chest was forced outward by the backward motion of his arms. His nipples seemed to be in a position of utter offering. His hips were jutting forward, carrying with them his cock and balls. His legs were slightly spread in a manner similar to any I would have a slave assume. I wouldn't have tolerated those thighs protecting his balls and neither would his drill instructor.

Carl was obviously transported by the experience. His cock was stiffening. His face was actually relaxing. He was, at last, back with a commander. That, he'd told me, was the one thing that was always necessary in his life. He had found it in the military. The Army had shown him how desperately he had wanted a sergeant to rule over him. But then, when he'd tried to express just how wonderfully important that was to him, it had ended. A dishonorable discharge and a nightmare of civilian life.

So, he decided, he would have to recreate his military existence. If the Army didn't want him as he was, he would discover people who did. The leather bars were his salvation. He had described his ecstasy when he'd walked into the first one. There were uniformed men. At least some of them were willing to command. With their discipline, he could structure the rest of his existence.

He'd become engulfed in the life it had offered. Suddenly no longer lost, he had a milieu that functioned for him. He had gotten a job. His needs were so minimal — as I could see in this apartment — that he was actually now, at the age of twenty-nine, fairly comfortable. He used his excess income to travel, always seeking more leather, more uniforms, more quasi-military events and situations.

I only wished that Martin's magic training camp still existed. Carl would have fit in, perfectly. It was made for his dreams of a military existence that had value for his hard cock and willing ass. But he was doing admirably well in reconstructing all of that for himself.

Discipline was the main goal in his sexual life. With it, he had enough for his other needs. But his demands had increased, not in terms of quantity, but of quality. There weren't many men who could carry out the fantasy with him in either of the ways he needed it: either to be perfectly aware of every detail of military life, or else, to be perfectly in command through other means.

I reached into the back rear pocket of my khaki pants and brought out a length of black leather, about an inch and a half wide. This was the symbol of my command. He had expected it. My movement brought about the first visible distraction from his perfect carriage. His eyes darted to my leather strap. "Eyes front," I spat out.

I stood back a couple feet. His body was in fine shape. He had only a slight bit of chest hair. The kinky curls were small, dark swirls on his chocolate skin. His pubic hair was much more full. His cock and balls, a deeply dark color of mixed purple and brown, were in perfect proportion to the rest of his body.

I went back to my chair. "My understanding is this: you're prepared to serve at my party on Sunday and on this evening. You understand that your role is strictly that of a plebe. You will respond to every order with perfect discipline and you understand that every failing is to be rewarded with the expected result."

"Yes, *sir!*"

"My standing orders were for your ass to be lubricated. Has that been done?"

"Yes, *sir!*"

"Are the supplies here?"

"Yes, *sir!*"

"You don't look in very good shape, Carl. Have you been fucking off on your exercises."

He was trapped. That look of fear took over again. He searched madly through his mind to find an answer that wouldn't offend me.

"I thought so. Hit the floor. Fifty push ups. *Now!*"

He dove for the floor. I sat and watched as he mechanically counted out the exercises. He had told me his work out regime. This wasn't going to be all that strenuous for him — unless he'd done them just before I'd arrived, hoping to impress me with his body. But, apparently not. He went through the movements with remarkable speed — and grace. Only towards the end, still counting off each repetition, did he begin to show the slightest strain that I could hear in his voice.

When he was finished, he stood up. His chest was expanding and contracting. He resumed his parade rest.

"Two more."

He started for a second. Before he got lost in his confusion, I went further.

"One to let you kiss each of my boots."

He moved quickly to comply. The two push ups were done with even more grace then the others. With each dip down, his lips touched my boots and lingered there, just for enough time to let me know that he was performing the required actions with sufficient appreciation.

When he stood up this time his cock was in full erection. The strap was still in my hands. I lifted it up to head level and stretched it between my clenched fists. I brought the tightly pulled leather closer to him. He didn't move until it was touching his lips. "Kiss it."

Not losing his ramrod posture, he did. His pursed lips were sensual as they moved, in total contradiction to the military stance he had taken, to caress the leather. I moved the strap back and forth, letting a foot-long length rub against his lips sensually. He never stopped his attention. His eyes closed, almost in ecstasy.

I remembered that drill instructors almost always have their charges kiss some element of their uniform as part of their indoctrination. I must have discovered some deeply held fetish of Carl's, one so far into his mind that he hadn't even known to tell me about it.

He was being taken into some kind of sexual extreme, far, far away from any I had thought I was taking him.

There was a sudden and tremendous shudder that tore through his body, forcing his shoulder and his chest to quiver and so powerfully gripping him that I expected him to fall over.

We both stood there silently. He opened his eyes. They were displaying obvious shock at what had happened. I reached down and felt the still warm discharge of his come on my pants. I scrapped it off with my palm and brought it up and smeared it on his face. He stood there and took it all.

"You'll pay for that." I said.

"Yes, *sir!*" he responded. I believed him. I believed him enough that I had to smile and he did too.

"You're going to get fucked good and hard for that — coming without permission. And you're going to make one hell of a slave at my party."

"Sir, with all due respect, I don't have a moment's doubt that it's all true." His smile broadened. "Permission to proceed getting the officer's condom, *sir.*"

"Granted."

Questions

"How was your dinner with Phil?"

Madame looked up from her lunch and glared at me. "As though that's the most important topic of conversation! I'm much more interested in your news."

"I'll get to that soon enough. Come on, tell me about your dinner. Once I get started neither one of us will think to get back to it."

"It was delightful. We went to the Top of the Mark, as I had planned. I dressed for him, in my most formal gown. He was perfectly attired. We acted as though we were ancient lovers, recapturing some moment in the South of France from decades ago. We laughed and gossiped. We talked about everything.

"Some of the waiters recognized him and — of course — the service was even more exquisite than it would have been otherwise. They took wonderful care of us. Once they heard our conversation ... Hah! The service could have been rivaled by Old Russia. Every busboy in the place wanted to hear what outrageous story he or I would tell next. They hung on his gossip of writers and artists and the most *interesting* proclivities of theirs that he'd observed over the years.

"I, needless to say, had a few things to add of my own. At the end, they bought us a bottle of awfully fine champagne, as though we had performed just for them."

"Which you adored."

"Which I — of course — adored. It really was a splendid rendezvous."

"Did you get any of them to attend to your rooms?"

"No." I'd caught her in something. I could watch her decide whether or not to admit to her actions. "I had plans for later in the evening."

"Who?"

"What, is more like it," she smiled. She was finished with her crepe and sat back in her chair, carefully dabbing at her lips. "A fine young man from one of the more, shall we say, prestigious publishing houses. I got him on recommendation from a friend in London. He's English, but working in New York now. I had to come to California to find him.

"His interests are very common among the English, especially the upper classes, and this one is certainly from there. I had brought my canes, as you'd imagine I would. I had him over my footstool with his shirttails up and his pants down and left all that near-porcelain skin the British have with some delightful red welts.

"I do think, sometimes, that none of them ever got over their experiences at public school. They seek to recreate them so often and with such . . . intensity."

We laughed over that, long and hard. It was true, we'd both seen it so often. While one wonders about the complex psychologies of American men and how they ever did get to the places that some of them have achieved, the English are so totally directed towards frequent and sound beatings that one can forget they ever do anything else. They love nothing more than a good, strong arm to take care of their backsides.

"I hope you got more than just the use of your canes," I said.

"Yes, but that wasn't really satisfactory. I would much rather be taking part in the roles of our fiction than simply fucking. That's all I could think of with this boy. He's thirty-five years old, but highly uncreative. I wanted to be some Amazon Queen, or one of your famous executive women who become natural dominatrices. Hell, I wanted to be my own creation, Madame. But, no. It was strictly tame.

"But, enough of this. I want the details of your activities. I'm so excited to think you might actually be making progress. It really is going to happen, isn't it?"

"Martin's here."

My comment made her freeze. She picked up her water glass

as though she needed a prop to take in the news. "Martin," she whispered. She sighed then, "Are you taking him back to New England with you?"

"No, no. He's here for the party. He lives in Los Angeles now. Doing well enough. He's becoming a top."

"Martin!?" It wasn't just that she was shocked, she was angry as well. "What does that mean?" She slammed her glass down on the table.

"It means that he's moving on, at least with other men."

"You fucked him last night, I presume?"

"No."

"How could you have Martin here and not fuck him? Oh, my god," her hand went to her chest as though she'd just thought a dreadful thought, "He didn't fuck *you*?"

"I'm not going to play at being a virgin after all these years," I said.

"When you were a child. Not while you've been such a man."

"This is beside the point. No. We didn't have sex — in the usual sense — last night. We each had an assignment. I was out interviewing someone for the party. Martin was applying some of his new-found skills as a disciplinarian to a particularly difficult recruit of ours, one of those who needs to get the humiliation and and abuse he desires if he's going to be useful later on."

"How could you two go on as though it had never happened?"

"Because it did happen, and it exists for us. But, really, the chapter is over. Not the stuff that stays with me — and him. Not the most perfect parts of it, the knowledge that he's always there, always going to show up again and again and be as wonderful as the last time. But it wouldn't work to drag him away.

"We always use the term 'boy' in our conversations. We both know that has nothing to do with age. Your own, last night, was nearly as old as I am. Martin — if this helps you — is an adolescent. He needs to grow away from his parents. In a certain sense, that's the two of us. Like some nineteen-year-old going off to college, he needs to create his own networks, become independent of his family, learn his own lessons.

"It doesn't deny his patrimony to make those kinds of decisions and to take those routes. It only means he's growing up. When he's older, he might very well come back again, like so many other sons, and take up residence next door, renew his position.

"Martin needed things, he needed me at one point and he needs not to have me now."

"But what will you do?"

"Madame, it is not the only love of my life. You care only because you saw it as something terribly special, which it is. Simply because it was the one S&M relationship that worked so well..."

"For so long," she insisted on adding.

"Yes, yes, it did work for a long time. But it was never fully traditional. We lived together for a very short time in there."

"But it was so beautiful."

"But there will be others, and in the meantime, Martin hasn't really left me. You must believe that."

"You should be settled down." She was becoming schoolmarmish on me again.

"I? Perhaps, someday, in a way. But the boys like Martin aren't what I necessarily want or need for that. I'm part of his network, his family. Much like you are for me. It all works for me, the sense of belonging and the sense of having others belong. That's my need now. I know he exists, and some of the others from this party will exist. Don't try to impose all the traditional structures on this existence. You and I are not here in this world to have church weddings in formal dress."

"I suppose not," she said.

The waiters came and cleared the empty plates from the table. We ordered coffee and made plans to return to the convention floor. It was all going to be tedious business. We tried to cheer ourselves up by daydreaming about certain personalities we knew at the party. The one editor who had been the subject of so many fantasies wasn't included in this conversation, as though we left him in a more honored space where it wouldn't be possible to joke about him. But there were many others we could imagine.

"That one stupid bitch who rejected your last book could use a bit of cane," Madame said.

"But, my dear, you're slipping. You know my thoughts in general, my philosophies as they've matured. This party's participants — in all their roles — should be there for good reasons. The need to serve, to display themselves, to enjoy the sensuous nature of bondage and the strap — those are the reasons they should have been chosen. To use this simply for punishment doesn't work. To squander all this art as though it was a way to get back at someone isn't appropriate at all."

"You can be such a purist," she said, but in a tone that conveyed appreciation, not rebuke. "You lose yourself so often in the world of your books — your own and Adrienne's. You two, wanting the fine world of masterful princes and their lovely charges..."

"A wonderful thought, to lift oneself up out of the gutter where this world insists that sex must be housed," I retorted. "It is a fine thought, to remove the ugly noises from sex and to find those jeweled places where it can exist."

"You would have had such a marvelous household in another time."

"Probably, my dear, only in the time of my fantasies."

"But you insist on creating them here, now, in this place as well." She stood up; it was time to leave. I joined her and took her arm. We walked out of the dining room and out of the hotel, moving towards the convention.

"It's like this gathering," I took up the conversation when we were out in the sunlight. "Everything around us is so defiled by corruption in one way or another. We're brought down to some low common denominator by it all, our sex is and so is our writing.

"Our finest moments, Madame, are in our minds and in our words. It's so seldom that we're able to translate them into our lives, no matter how much we try.

"You get upset about Martin, by my not keeping him forever and by his leaving. But, of course, I have my moment with Martin. He's like the finest paragraph I've ever written, my masterpiece. To go beyond him and the others with whom I've gotten that far is such an astonishing idea."

"Oh, but I remember when you thought you'd never write what you do. I remember when you and Martin lived in the far north together, creating an epic novel with your lives. That was taken from you — so sad, so tragic. But you began that epic. Someday, you know, you will try it again. I want to be there and see that happen."

"But you must remember," I said, "we didn't finish that one together and when I do write the next one, it might not be Martin who's the collaborator."

"But the attempt, the simple fact of the attempt, will be awesome."

An Interruption

"You want to do what!?" I was incredulous. Martin was standing in the hotel room with his arms defiantly crossed over his chest.

"You heard me. I want to make my own contribution."

"Your contribution is going to be getting your ass beaten to a pulp!"

"Please, let me do this one thing. I know you've already made plans for me for this fucking party of yours. All right, I know how important it is that I perform well for you. I'll do it. I promise I'll do anything you want there. But I want to bring my own slave to the party."

"You don't even have one to bring! You don't know the men in San Francisco any more. You think you're going to get dressed in your show-off leather and waltz down to Folsom Street and find someone who'd be perfect for my party? You're crazy."

"That muscle-bound closet case you got yourself tied up with is hardly a catch."

"You know why I'm having him at the party."

"Yeah, sure, he's living beauty. You forgive that kind of man so many things, a few muscles and a pretty face and you start relaxing those inflated standards of yours."

"The party's at least partially a visual event."

"Fine. I could have carried that off for you. I'm not exactly a troll. You said this black guy was handsome, the blond kid from Colorado's cute. The couple's hot. You didn't need to add Christopher."

"Are you going to tell me that you didn't enjoy your little tryst with him last night?"

"I had a fine time. But it was one of those masturbatory things — the ones you told me about. There was nothing to it but the body. His mind is trapped in deepest Ohio..."

"The same state you happen to be from."

"And the one I left to live with you."

"Enough of this. Christopher is beautiful. We agree. He'll be getting precisely what he wants from the party and he'll appear exquisite. The others will more than make up for him. But your street tricks..."

"I won't bring back a street trick."

"You sound like some puppy dog that wants to give his master a present and doesn't understand that the master isn't exactly delighted with a dead field mouse."

He threw his hands in the air. He tried once more. "*Please*, just let me try, for once."

I played back all of my conversation with Madame about him and finally shrugged a very resigned agreement. "Fine. If you have to prove something to me, then go ahead and do it. I'm not at all sure about this, but you know that."

"Yes, I do." He was jubilant. I realized suddenly that he hadn't really expected to win. I could have held out longer and won the argument. But it was done.

"You'll have hell to pay if you fail."

"It's Saturday night in San Francisco. How can I fail to find a perfect trick on Folsom Street?"

That made me laugh. I was remembering years ago and the far from perfect encounters I'd had. "Get out. You certainly have your work to do."

He was dressed in full leather, chaps over his leather pants; jacket, vest, shirt, all of them were leather; his boots were highly polished. He put on his cap. "And I do still know people here. Enough to find what we need."

"You have the rest of it all set up? The food's being delivered? All the tools you'll need? The bar..."

"All of it. I promise."

"Then, go on. I have my last appointment to keep."

He kissed me and bounded out the doorway.

* * *

My own activities were going to call for markedly different clothes than Martin's leather. I dressed carefully in a three-piece suit, the finest I owned. My best shoes and an especially well-designed silk tie were part of the outfit. So was the most extravagant set of jewelry — cufflinks, tie stud — that I owned. My newest recruit would appreciate all of the details.

Francois's apartment wasn't far away, it was on the top of the hill, in one of the finer buildings. I arrived and my appearance met with the obvious approval of the observant doorman. He called up for me and then retrieved the elevator that took me to the appropriate floor.

Francois was waiting at his doorway. "Sir, a pleasure." He stood back, graciously holding the door open. While the other men I'd met had often been clumsy in their attempts to discover how they should greet my arrival, Francois knew exactly what the correct moves were. He bowed deeply at the waist as I passed by him.

I entered into an impeccably decorated apartment. It was small. I could see there wasn't even a bedroom. The upholstered couch had to fold out for a sleeping space. I took an offered chair and studied my surroundings. Every single item was superb. The china ashtrays I recognized as Limoges. The crystal was an assortment of the finest from Czechoslovakia and Belgium. The small tables were all covered in handworked leather.

"Would the maitre care for an aperitif?" Francois spoke flawless English. There was only a hint of an accent left in his voice. It made the use of his term for "Master" all the more impressive. He was standing in front of me. He was wearing a waiter's tuxedo, its creases sharp and the shirt crisply starched.

"Please."

He bowed again and seemed to be moving toward the small kitchen, whose entrance was only partially hidden by an antique folding screen of some oriental origin, probably Chinese. But he stopped just short of the door. He carefully took off his jacket and deliberately hung it over a large valet's stand.

In his shirt, he proceeded to go into the other room and quickly returned with a small glass of Byrrh in which floated a beautifully cut sliver of lemon peel. It was delivered to me on a small silver tray he held in the palm of his hand.

"If the maitre will excuse me, I must see to his dinner's

preparation."

I nodded my dismissal. While he quietly and efficiently moved through his tasks I watched the little glimpses of his body I could get from the space between the screen and the door frame.

He was a perfectly pleasant looking man. I had suspected he was thirty or so. I realized that he had taken such extremely good care of himself and his appearance that he could be older.

He had written to me saying that he was a steward on an international airline. He'd been living out that fantasy of mine concerning the perfect service that airline personnel could give if only our mores weren't so stupid. While he certainly hadn't gone about his duties in chains and hadn't — so far as he would admit — performed actual sexual acts on board, his dreams were fulfilled by the very role of being a servant to the travellers who were his charge.

I sipped the Byrrh, enjoying its plum flavor, and it seemed that he timed his reappearance precisely with the moment when I'd finished the drink.

"Your appetizer." He bowed less formally this time, but with no less meaning than he had before.

I went to the table and allowed him to pull out my chair for me. On the plate in front of me was a delicate duck paté, nicely formed and served with some fine crackers of a sort I'd never had before. While I began to taste the delicious morsel, Francois came in with a small split of white wine which he carefully poured into one of the array of glasses in front of me.

I only happened to notice that his shoes were gone. I was startled at first. Then, with a smile I tried very hard to keep to myself, I understood his game. If he was going to be able to carry it off as well as he was accomplishing this meal, I wouldn't interfere.

A well-made, light soup followed, and with it, Francois's socks disappeared. His cummerbund went with the serving of a palate cleanser, a sharply flavored raspberry sorbet. He must have considered this an informal meal, there was no fish course. But the entree — a delectable small beefsteak that he'd sauteed perfectly and served with a delicate cognac sauce — meant that there was no longer a shirt either.

Like many French men, Francois's body hair didn't really extend up onto his chest. Instead it gathered in a rich swirl around his belly. His nipples were unprotected, dark colored pieces of hard flesh. They'd obviously seen a great deal of use, they stuck out with as much invitation as the tiny roasted potatoes that had come with my meat.

When the white wine had been cleared and he brought on the split of rich Lafite-Rothschild, Francois appeared wearing only his black bow tie and his small French styled briefs. They were a bright yellow color, flyless, made of a particularly soft cotton that held his obviously enlarged cock and balls in a smooth pouch.

During the service, we both ignored his utterly perfect strip. Each article of clothing was carefully stored on its place on the valet. He appeared at my side for each service with all seriousness. If anything, his attention and sobriety increased as the clothing left.

He didn't bother me with the ridiculous banter of American waiters. The food was simply served and our conversation was that of a baron and his butler. "Was the maitre's journey pleasant?" "Will the maitre care for more wine?" "May I take the maitre's plate?" "Are the maitre's plans progressing well?"

At least I was able to anticipate the final scene. My dessert, a chocolate mousse, arrived in the hands of my host who was now dressed only in his correctly attired bow tie. I'm sure that my ability to ignore his progression added to his excitement. Once his cock was free of even the briefs, it was half hard.

I finished and sat back in my chair, a hand on my stomach signaling my appreciation of what he'd prepared for me.

"Will the maitre take his coffee in the sitting area?"

"Yes."

He pulled the chair back for me. I couldn't help but graze his cock as I moved past him. He sucked in his breath quickly and whispered, "I'm very sorry, maitre."

In my chair, I was served a cup of fine coffee. The tray was again silver, only larger. The cup, saucer, creamer and sugar bowl were all of the same pattern.

"The maitre must be very tired from all of the work involved with his party. Perhaps I could relax him."

It wasn't a question, more of a statement of intent. Francois knelt in front of me and carefully removed my shoes and socks. He began to massage my feet with a skill that could never have been anticipated. His fingers seemed to dance over my skin, never making a wrong move, always finding the tender areas that could use his careful ministrations.

This, obviously, was his desire. I thought of Phil's great and joyful fetish for men's feet. I would have to make sure that he and Francois had an opportunity to spend some time together to explore their mutual interests. Francois's metal-hard cock certainly was all the proof I needed that he was, indeed, in his private ecstasy. His heavy French foreskin still covered the head of his cock, giving it a smoother look than erections usually have.

"The maitre is enough pleased to allow Francois to attend the party?"

"It appears that you have more than adequate skills to make that worthwhile."

He leaned over and elegantly kissed the tops of each of my feet. "I have a special love for food, maitre. Is there, at this late date, some way I could help in that particular area?"

"The materials have been ordered. But, of course, you could be assigned that role, if you choose."

"I would be honored." His hands were still massaging me. "Your plate and silver service, the flatware..."

"From the hotel."

He froze, almost in horror. "Common commercial goods for your party? Maitre, please, I have so much here, of the finest quality. I've dreamed of your party since I first heard of it. To have it be less than perfect is something I couldn't stand. Mightn't I please..."

"But the party is tomorrow afternoon. There's not enough time."

"If you'd allow me to perhaps visit your rooms tonight, I could take an inventory. I could come back with some help and get everything that could ever be needed here. I could review the food and drink and make sure that some slight thing that I could have provided from my own stores wouldn't be necessary. I..."

"Francois, yes. I can see that you not only have the knowledge but the ... passion for this. Yes. Come to my suite and see what's available. I'll have at least one boy there in the early morning who can help you. Now, put my shoes and socks back on. Get dressed. I know good talent when I see it."

"Maitre," he leaned forward one more time and kissed my feet again.

In his street clothes, Francois looked more like a French sailor than an elegant steward. He wore tight pants, but with an air of great masculinity. I had thought that he might have been somewhat effeminate in his day-to-day clothes, but while there was certainly a grace in his walk that reminded me of a ballet dancer, the image of his broad shoulders was intensified in his clinging short-sleeved shirt.

He was absorbed in his role. There was not a hint that he wanted to give up a single part of it. He opened the doors, always bowing his head. He never initiated a conversation. He walked a perfect half step behind me at as we made our way to my hotel.

I had to unlock the door to let him in. It was late, the dinner had been long and leisurely. Martin had already returned. More than that, he had come back with his prey. Francois and I didn't wake them when we came into the suite. The two of them were sleeping on the couch; it had folded out to provide a double bed.

Martin was on his side with his back to us. His heavy arm was resting on a smaller body. I walked up, as quietly as possible, and looked over to see a nicely built young man asleep. There was an intricate rope harness wrapped around him. I could tell that it held him immobile. The bondage — I recognized it as a kind of art that the Japanese had been the most successful with — was complete. There was this young man, held at the same time by two forces: A man who had claimed him with lust and the rope the man had demanded.

Francois whispered in my ear: "Are they yours?"

"One used to be," I said, suddenly very sad.

We went to the bed room. Francois announced, "You're tired. The planning has been so much, making all these boys do the right thing! You must need a bath."

He immediately went to draw it. While it was pouring, he came back in and gently began to undress me, performing his valet's duties with the same dignity as he had everything else that night. I was tired. I let him go on and eventually lead me into the bathroom.

I sank into the water which was at a perfect temperature.

Francois had brought a small pouch with him. I had assumed it was simply those things a man might have when he is to spend the night with another, and I hadn't paid it any attention. But now he brought it into the bathroom and emptied it out on the sink's shelf. He brought out some kind of salt which he poured into the bath. The odor from it was solid, masculine and still very pleasant.

Then he took some kinds of tools I wasn't very familiar with at first. I recognized them but couldn't remember ... Of course, they were the implements necessary for a pedicure. My Francois was not about to stop with a minor indulgence in his foot fetish. This was an *artiste!*

I actually slumbered off while his hands worked on my feet, seeming to find their own special pleasure in my toes. I hadn't had anyone pay so very much attention to those small parts of my anatomy in quite a while. I certainly hadn't had so very much expertise focused on them. I seemed to fall into a soft and welcome sleep.

I woke up with a bit of a start. It couldn't have been that long, my skin was still smooth. I had been roused by a strange smell. I looked down and saw that Francois, who had undressed during my nap, was applying the last touches of a plain nail polish to my nails. My toes — such a woefully ignored part of one's body — seemed suddenly very beautiful. His work had been even better than I had thought it might.

He looked up at me while he replaced the top to the polish container. He was smiling, just as pleased as I was with the results. He went back to work, blowing gently to speed up the drying. When he was convinced that the job had been done, he stood up. His cock was again in its full erection.

I climbed out of the bath, trying not to be awkward as I kept my polished toes out of the water. He was waiting with a towel, and immediately went to work drying me. He knew precisely how to be gentle while still applying enough pressure that I understood that a man was doing the labor.

I felt wonderfully cared for. The meal, the wine and brandy, the bath and the tingling on my feet were all combined in one totally self-indulgent sensation.

He led me casually into the bedroom. He pulled back the covers with great precision. I sat down on the edge. "If the maitre will permit me to spend the night, I could perform my duties more adequately in the morning."

"Of course." I looked at him carefully. His head was bent far over, his eyes looking straight at the floor. His cock was rampant. "But you'll sleep at the foot of the bed, on the floor."

"Of course, maitre."

"Chained to the bed."

"If the maitre wishes."

"After you've spent your time at my feet."

He looked up. I recognized the expression. It was almost a desperation. He was wondering if I really understood what he wanted. If I did, a dream could be fulfilled.

I stood up and went to my bags. I quickly found what I wanted. I told him to arranged the extra sheets and blankets on the floor by one of the legs of the bed. He did. I returned and placed a heavy metal collar around his neck. I took its attached chain and padlocked it to the bed. He was forced by the chain's short length to get on his hands and knees. He looked up at me, his mouth open, his eyes nearly tearing. He was so close to what he wanted.

"Flat on your stomach." I gave the order with a quiet authority, not the shouting I had used with Carl. Francois fell onto his belly. I moved closer. I forced one of my feet underneath his face. "Make love to me."

He actually cried out in some mixture of pain and delight. His two hands cradled my foot. His mouth opened and his tongue licked and sucked at me. The hands were moving and grasping and clutching and adoring all at once. His hips were moving rapidly against his makeshift bed. It took a very few seconds before his whole body was seized with a tremor. His ass, beautifully hairy as French asses so often are, quivered, his legs shook.

Then there was no more power in his hands. His head fell on my foot and rested there for a moment, only making the slightest movements to rub a little bit against me.

"Thank you, maitre. Thank you, forever."

"Go to sleep. You have a lot of work to do in the morning."

The Morning

I woke up first. I was amazingly refreshed. It seemed my feet were the first part of me to become conscious. My soles, my ankles, my toes were all tingling with a special delight. Francois, of course. I smiled. I indulge in so many parts of my own and other men's bodies but I hadn't remembered what special and lingering pleasure feet can be.

I stood up, stretched, and moved to the end of the bed. Francois was curled up there. I stood and looked at him, wondering what was the balance between the physical discomfort of his position and the mental joy? I nudged at his chest with a foot. He stirred, momentarily confused, but seemed to remember where he was quickly. He sat up so fast that he tugged at his chain. I had the key in my hand and reached down to unlock him.

He rubbed his neck where the metal must have chafed against it and then jumped to his feet. He had a healthy morning erection swinging in front of him. Typically, he ignored it.

"Your bath, maitre."

He rushed past me and into the bathroom. I followed and in a short while was once again in the embrace of the warm water. He was moving quickly now, all business. He left me in the water and I could only vaguely hear him. I thought he was rummaging through the things in the front room that Martin had brought home.

"Maitre, *it will not do!*"

I looked up at him standing over me with his hands on his waist.

"None of it is good enough. I need both of those boys this

morning. We will have to go to my apartment at once and collect *everything*."

I sat there, stunned for a moment. "Fine, it's your responsibility. Wake them up after you've dried me off." I got out of the water and Francois went about his duties to my body, much less gently than he had last night. But he wasn't going to shirk any of them. He had carefully gotten out what he must have decided to be the appropriate clothes for a master at leisure, and dressed me. Only then did he storm out of the bedroom and into the front room.

I heard him clapping his hands loudly and yelling, "Up, up, there's work to do."

A barely awake Martin answered, "What the fuck ... Who the fuck..."

"Our maitre's party is in danger. Up!"

There was a highly articulate exchange of swear words then between the two of them, some sounds that must have been made by the other younger man who I hadn't met, and a rush of noises that told me Martin was getting dressed. Francois was winning his battle.

I had expected them to come into the bedroom and argue in front of me. But it didn't happen. In a few minutes the door to the room slammed shut and there was silence.

I wasn't about to leave the suite; I didn't want to miss a single thing that might happen next. I called the front desk and asked for Joseph. He called back in a few minutes. I gave him a short list of things to get me — just some rolls, juice and coffee along with the Sunday newspapers. I had no intention of eating the hotel fare and gave him specific instructions on where to shop.

He arrived in a short while. He carrying in the parcels and the paper and put them on the coffee table.

"Been having fun?"

The room was littered with some of the reminders of Martin and his friend. The leather was scattered all over the place. Obviously Martin had decided against wearing it out on a Sunday morning and must have had other clothes nearby. The long pieces of rope he had used to tie up his trick were thrown over the back of the couch.

I didn't say anything to him. I just opened the bags and began to pull out my food.

"Leather. Real kinky. Like you said you were. What you going to do, man? Have your slaves all tied up, have little leather boys running around with their asses all beat and shit?" He was laughing. I didn't say a word or respond at all. His smile disappeared. "You are, aren't you? Jesus, man. You really are."

I opened up the newspaper. "Thanks for the errand, Joseph."

Before he could say anything more or leave, the door opened and Francois came in, leading the way for Martin and his companion. All three of them were burdened with boxes, and shopping bags dangled from their hands.

"Carefully, *carefully,*" Francois was insisting as the others put down their loads.

He didn't stop to acknowledge me or Joseph. "You," he said to Martin, "Move that shit out of the way. Put it in some closet."

He was pointing to the things Joseph had gotten out of the hotel stores. "Hey, man, that's my responsibility," Joseph shouted.

"Then get it out of here. As soon as possible. It's unbearable that you would have brought that here for the party. Have you no sense of nobility when you're in its presence? The maitre can't be having his guests eating off of that shit!"

Joseph was as dumbstruck as the rest of us. He was frozen in place for a moment, and then, angry, began to move. He went to the telephone and called for some help. he spoke in Spanish and I couldn't follow the conversation. "We'll get the stuff out of here. For Christ's sake, what kind of shit is this?"

"Joseph, here, for your trouble," I handed him another of the many bills he seemed to be collecting from me. It calmed him down considerably.

"Okay, okay. But I wish you'd made up your mind a lot earlier. Could have saved us a lot of trouble."

"It is not the maitre's duty to attend to such things. Now, move it, get this stuff out."

There was a knock on the door. When Joseph answered it there were two other young men there. He gave them some quick orders and a period of utter pandemonium broke out as his contingent went about one set of business and my own kept up its labor under Francois's sharp voiced command.

I ate my breakfast rolls and drank my coffee.

* * *

"Where the hell did you find that one?" Martin demanded a couple hours later.

I only smiled at him.

"He's worse than you ever were."

"That's because I was only so demanding in sex, which you always enjoyed. Even the little things I'd make you do around the house were always in an erotic context. You never had to experience the reality of slave labor.

"If you had, you would have realized that the most vicious overseers have always been other slaves."

"Tell me." He collapsed on the bed, his arms and legs spread out. "How do you like Sean?"

"He looks fine."

"Is that all?"

"More than that." It was true. Martin's find was quite handsome. He was a perfect match for Keith, in fact. They were the same short height and had the same young and hard build. I was already playing with those possibilities in my mind.

"Your French bastard had us up and out of here by nine this morning. It's already noon. What time is everyone due here?"

"Three."

"Do you have it well enough planned out?"

"Enough."

"The others? When do they arrive?"

"At one. You, your friend and Francois had better start showering, shaving, getting ready. Christopher's the first one due. You're going to have to work on him."

"How? I thought my little session with him was enough to get him in the mood. It sure seemed to be."

"Yes, but his body needs to be shaved. Especially close. You'll have to prepare him."

Martin sat up at that idea. It obviously appealed to him. "What else?"

"You'd better get Sean in here. I suppose he and I should meet and get a number of things clear between us."

"You're going to play with *my* boy?"

"I'm going to inspect *my* slave."

Martin wasn't quite willing to give everything up that easily. He got Sean to come into the bedroom, but didn't give me the time to start giving the young man any of the orders that he knew were going to be coming. "Strip." He gave the command himself with a sharpness that even I admired.

The young man with the reddish hair and the pale skin I'd seen earlier in the day hesitated, then began to move, looking at me with a touch of apprehension.

He was wearing jeans, boots, a black t-shirt. A leather jacket was now in the back of the hallway closet, put there by Francois so its sight wouldn't offend my guests.

The boy was extremely attractive naked. He had a complexion on his torso that betrayed his Irish heritage. There were hints of freckles all over, especially on his shoulders and the whole length of his arms. His belly was flat and his chest was full, though they would have appeared even more extreme if there had been any body hair to emphasize their lines. Sean had only a pale red growth over his cock and balls. His legs, his arms, all of the rest of him below the waist seemed to be as naturally nude as Christopher was shaven.

He stood there while I looked him over.

"I hope Martin had the sense to explain this to you, to let you know that this wasn't a game. I'm doing something very important. I'm allowing him to include you as a special favor to him. I hope you'll live up to his expectations."

"I heard what he said," Sean answered. He seemed to have an air of defiance about him. But of course! That was what would attract Martin.

"Where did you two meet?" I asked.

There was a smile building on Martin's face and a scowl on Sean's. Martin answered: "There was a wrestling night at one of the gay bars."

"And you won." I answered my own question. "But before the match, you made him agree to do whatever you wanted him to?"

"That was the deal." *Aren't I still your boy?*

"And you agreed — and still do?" I asked Sean. "Yeah."

"No! That's not good enough."

"I keep my word." Sean was staring at me, real fury on his face. "I told him whoever won got the guy for the next day — no holds barred, safe sex the *only* limit. The only limit. So he told me what it was. Okay? I'm here. I'm not going to leave. I heard about you. Not just from him. Some other guys at the bar were talking about you and your party. I'm no amateur, you know. I get around.

"There's not many people that don't know what you're doing. So, you got me. I understand."

"But do you understand?"

"I understand I lost a match to a guy. I understand I made a bet. I understand I gotta pay up. I keep my promises. You got it."

"But I need more than a petulant loser. I need someone who's going to give me the kind of submission that will make this party the event it has to be."

"If I'm not as good as anyone else, you got me for another day. I don't hedge on my bets."

"You shouldn't have said that so quickly," Martin teased him. "You should think what 'another day' might mean."

"I'll do it right," Sean said, a little less passionately. "I promise you. I'll do it right."

* * *

Everyone seemed to want to do things right. The knocks on the door to the suite began sounding precisely at one. Christopher was dressed in sports clothes. I was sure he realized nothing else was going to be necessary. He stood awkwardly and took in all the activity that was going on. I sent him off to the bathroom to be shaved.

"Martin," I called out as the two of them starting walking out of the front room. "All of it. I don't want a single strand beneath his neck."

Christopher blushed. He was, I'm sure, humiliated by the very idea. That was just as well. It would help him create a more appropriate mindset.

There was another knock on the door. I answered it. Glen and Phillip had arrived. They had a sheepish look on their faces. I slapped Glen's fine ass as he walked by. He yelped and turned quickly — too quickly. I stared at him until he shrugged and smiled. "Just a reminder, huh?"

"Only the first of many."

"Yes, sir." He said it with a nice mumble and a nicer blush. Phillip didn't need any reminder. He was looking around the room at the disarray and was anxious enough to ask what he could do to help.

Before I could answer, there was another knock. It was Keith. He came into the suite with a long stride. He had no hint of hesitation. He kissed me when I had closed the door, something I wasn't quite expecting. "I'm real excited."

"We'll see about that," I replied. The details were getting out of hand. It was time to take some control. "Francois, what do you need done?"

"Everything. *Everything!*" He said in a Gallic temper fit. He was pawing through the groceries that I had had Martin shop for.

This was enough. I walked up to him and grabbed him by the shirt collar. "Strip. Now."

He froze and then seemed to move to begin arguing again. I yanked once more at his shirt collar. "Strip."

"Maitre," he said, bowing his head.

"You three, get out of your clothes as well." Keith, Glen and Phillip joined Francois's undressing. Sean was over in the corner, vaguely playing with himself. "You get your hands off your cock. It's going to get more than enough attention today.

"Better, much better. Maybe you'll all get your minds back on what's happening here." Keith certainly was; his nice young cock was already swelling to an erection. "Now, get these clothes out of this room. There's a closet in the hallway. Francois, I'll ask you once more before I get out the strap, what needs to be done?"

"The table needs to be set. The dishes are all here now. I need to know who's going to be doing what, where everyone will be."

I explained my plan to him, being rewarded with his obvious esteem. "Beautiful, of course." Now he was satisfied that the plan was in hand. He went back to work in earnest.

In a few moments Carl arrived. I had him undress immediately. My entourage was complete. When Martin and a completely shorn Christopher entered the room, I checked the time and knew it was the moment to begin.

"Martin, I want him on his back over the cocktail table. His calves tied to one set of the table legs, his forearms to another. Not too tight. He'll be in that position for quite a while. Watch out for his circulation."

"Rope?"

"You'll find it in my black suitcase, as always."

Martin's years in the Navy had given him an intricate

knowledge of knots. His ability with bondage is well known. The rest of the boys watched as the huge bodybuilder was laid out over the table surface. He accepted his directions with an easy compliance. His muscles were not being strained, I could see that Martin was taking my orders seriously, but the position was allowing all of us to see the firmly etched development Christopher had achieved in his hours in the gymnasium.

Martin, knowing how important this was to me, did his work magnificently, using a long length of rope to achieve nothing less than a sculpture on Christopher's body, with some of the extra pieces crisscrossing his mammoth chest and emphasizing his pectorals. Christopher groaned, as though he understood this was a preamble to the bells, those wonderful hated bells that I had promised him.

"You," I turned to Glen and Phillip, "I want each of you standing with your backs to one of those pillars at the entrance of the sitting room. Put your arms behind you, behind the pillars, and your feet on either side of column."

I went into the bedroom and returned with four sets of leather restraints. "It's such a shame not to display those beautiful marks on your ass and back," I whispered to Glen as I went about my own work. "They look marvelous."

He didn't say anything at first, but then looked directly at me, "Thank you, sir."

"Don't you like them?" I asked as I placed the cuffs on each of his wrists and then joined them behind the column.

"Very much," he said, then smiled, "A lot."

"There'll be many more, I'm sure."

"I'm sure, too."

I bent down and put a matching set of cuffs on his ankles. I had placed hooks in the bottom on the pillars and used them now to attached his legs.

I repeated the process with Phillip. The actions I was performing and the sight of his lover only a few feet across from him had excited him. His cock was growing. I grabbed hold of it when I was done. "Save this, Phillip, you'll need to remember how much you're being turned on in a while."

He must have thought that the simple act of bondage was all I expected. There was a sudden panic on his face, "What else are you going to do?"

I kissed him and then said, "Anything I want to."

Carl was the easiest of the group. I had decided that to play to his military fantasy was the very easiest means of using him. He was naked now, but the only one with any piece of clothing at all on his handsome black body. A white metal military hat was on his head, a white belt around his waist. Tall military boots were on his feet. I didn't have to say a word to him. He had automatically assumed parade rest against the wall just inside the door to the suite. That was precisely where I wanted him.

Keith and Sean were next. Now that Martin had finished with Christopher I could put him to work on the two younger men. "A simple sculpture," I said. "Here, in front of the table. Have them kneeling, but absolutely immobilized, facing each other only a foot or so apart."

"You have some lengths of leather..."

"Whatever you choose. Create for me." I left him alone with his handiwork and went over to Francois who had been working at the food. In the other room there were hot plates to heat the water for tea as well as ice packs to cool the wine. I could see that Francois was working quickly with the basic ingredients we had on hand. The French genius was coming through. I tasted first one, then another of the things he had brought along and those he was making.

"Fine," I said. "This is going to do perfectly well."

* * *

It was done. It was all prepared. There were only the slightest touches left. I went back to my bags and brought out more implements. I went to Glen first. In my hand was a gag.

"You don't need that," he objected. There was no avoiding my intention.

"But I want it," I answered. I inserted the length of leather into his mouth. It was just large enough to fill him up, perhaps cause a little discomfort, but certainly not pain. More impressive was the intricate headband of leather straps that went with it. When I had finished my handiwork it was as though I had created a lattice around his head.

Phillip got precisely the same. I wanted them to be a perfectly matched pair. I stepped back and saw that they were.

Christopher got a similar, though simpler, gag. "You, at least, will need it." As soon as it was firmly attached I pulled out the despised tit clamps and their bells. He groaned, but through the gag the sound was just pleasant. As soon as the balls were attached I used my fingers to let play their little music for both my and his enjoyment.

Then I went further. His groans increased when he realized I had gone out and found more of the bells. I went quickly about the business of attaching two of them to his testicles and one of them to his cock. As though it was rebelling against his own desires, his erection stiffened at the humiliation and jerked upwards, forcing the bell to sound.

Perfect.

Martin's decoration of Keith and Sean was exquisite. It was — I'm sure purposely — overdone. They had no need for all the leather bands and rope that he'd used. It was all for the sake of ornamentation. They were on their knees, as I'd told him to place them. They were separated by just enough space to allow their cocks to barely touch — a very pretty sight.

I put very loose clamps on their nipples — not tight enough to cause any real pain, at least not for a while, but they wouldn't fall off, either. They were actually earrings. Small eyedrop-shaped pieces of mother of pearl drooped from their chests.

Glen and Phillip got their own nipple decorations: matching sets of gold rings that I'd found which left the impression that they were pierced. Glen overreacted and started to protest through his gag as soon as I had put them on him. But he must have realized he was helpless and soon gave up.

When I reached for Carl's nipples he stiffened. "They still hurt from the other night?"

"Yes, sir."

"They'll feel even better tomorrow." I had found very plain metal decorations for his chest, masculine in a way that fit his bearing.

"Thank you, sir," he said. He was looking down at them, wondering, I think, what they were doing on his body. They were a silver-looking metal, brightly polished, and the small half-moon they formed under each of his tits made his chest look perfect.

"The rest of it," I said to Martin. "A glass of wine," I told Francois. I went and sat in my chair and waited for my guests to arrive, pleased beyond description at my handiwork.

Madame, of course, was first. She was wonderfully dressed. She had on a top made of some metallic fabric which clung to her breasts. Her makeup was flawless. I had once criticized her for her choices in powder and coloring and from that day on she's always spent hours on her face before showing herself to me at an occasion like this one.

I watched to see how my plan worked. At her knock, Martin had opened the door. He'd bowed. He motioned her into the room, not saying a word even though they knew one another. Carl stepped forward and took her coat for her. Martin then escorted her past Glen and Phillip to where I was standing waiting to greet her. In a moment Francois was beside us with a glass of white wine in a handsome crystal glass which he carried on a gold tray.

Madame sat down before she could respond. "Perfect."

I smiled and took my own seat back. The men were all naked. All of them were erect. I had sent Martin through them and had him place the black condoms on each one instructing him to suck the covered cocks hard if required — but that hadn't been necessary.

My orders were explicit: Each one of them had to be hard and Martin had to keep them hard with his mouth. He could use his hand only on himself. Christopher wouldn't be a problem; he was the only one with an unsheathed cock. I only had to put a finger on its extended length if I thought it was going to soften. I did that now, just to tease Madame.

But Christopher's cock wasn't the thing that was impressing her. What she was studying so deeply was the food arranged over his body. A pate was placed perfectly on his abdomen; a cheese preparation was on the shaved area where his pubic hair would have been; pieces of fruit surrounded the outlines of his pectorals; stalks of fresh vegetables rose up from beside his testicles and underarms.

He was the centerpiece to our banquet.

Then Phil arrived. I watched as he came and took in the scene. Now quite old, he still had all the handsome features on his face that had sent their messages into the minds and bodies of men and women in Europe, North America, all over the world, when he'd been a younger man.

I'd once seen a photograph taken when he'd been in his twenties, living in Paris between the Wars and being kept by some of the most wealthy aristocrats who clustered to the French capital in those days. He was standing against an alley wall, wearing a kind of disreputable t-shirt that marked the Apache toughs, a cigarette dangling from the side of his mouth as he half-smiled, half-sneered at the camera.

That same expression was on his face now, decades later. It was proof of the perseverance of his sexual being that age hadn't defeated it at all. He was staring hardest at Carl. The combination of race and military artifacts would have touched him much more than the rest.

But, whatever else, Phil is a gentleman. He came across the room to greet Madame, trying not to appear to linger too long at the sight of the naked men tied to pillars or bound on their knees on the floor.

He kissed her hand elegantly, then stood and shook mine. He glanced down at Christopher and lost control of the leer that was bursting to get outside him. "You son of a bitch," he said to me. He ran a hand over Christopher's impressive torso and used a finger to lick a bit of pate from his belly. Then he laughed out loud. "You goddamn son of a bitch."

"Tea, Francois."

That caught Phil's attention. He watched as Francois walked back into the room carrying his tea on that same golden serving tray. When the naked servant reached him he broke into a torrent of his fluent French that was too fast for either Madame or me to follow.

I could only hear that Francois was using "Maitre" to Phil as frequently as he did to me. I could also tell that there was something going on that appealed to both men. Certainly Francois's cock wasn't going down.

"Do you know him?" I finally asked.

"Think, think, of course we know of each other. I've wanted to meet him for quite some time. Evidently his specialty is so intense that he's not going to mind indulging an ancient man like myself..."

Of course! Phil adored feet as well. I could suddenly see that

Francois would be willing to cross the Bay and give the old man some intense pleasure. I felt a new wave of pleasure, happy to have made any connection between the men. Just the idea of having the pleasure — the honor — of making a match between Phil and someone who would deliver sexual delight to him was wonderful.

And then, of course, Adrienne arrived.

I had been worried, so had Madame. But Adrienne entered the room with the same confidence and energy that she had when she did anything. There was, I think, a slight hesitation when the door was opened and my tall, muscular Martin was there, his erection standing straight out from his body. But she was not going to show that to us.

The boys went through their duties, carefully taking her coat, bringing her into the other guests. When she sat down and pulled out one of her omnipresent unfiltered cigarettes, Martin was on the spot with a light for her. She dragged in on it, leaned back in her chair and exhaled a cloud of smoke with great melodrama. "Remarkable."

I looked at Martin and saw more than a little appreciation in his face as he studied her. He was never one to limit himself just to men and the sight of the stately trim and blond Adrienne, so perfectly dressed, was something that he would admire.

I wouldn't have possibly cross-examined Adrienne on her reactions to the party and the men. It wouldn't have been right. She had understood perfectly well that this was, in its way, a gift to her. Just the sight, just the experience of the naked men serving, was something that I knew she would admire for many years, forever.

And, I had to admit, they were wonderfully attractive and attentive. Martin wouldn't have let me down, as much for his own pride as anything else. His fat cock was dripping inside its sheath, we could all see the milky liquid building up inside it, a sharp contrast to the black latex.

Christopher was in agony. But the agony of his hugely muscled body was beautiful to see. He attempted to move around in the tight bounds, just trying to have some change in position. Each maneuver he made highlighted another set of muscles. We all made sure that there was constant attention to him, I caught Madame and Phil both pinching and squeezing at his more vulnerable parts when they ostensibly were reaching for a piece of food.

Martin was going about his duties. With that kind of serious intent that he has about sex, he made the rounds of the tied-up slaves and sucked each of them, making their condoms glisten with sex those times that they didn't need to be made more erect. There was a constant sound of his slight sucking. But we all understood this was no simple sex show. The fact was that one man was mouthing the rest of them, not for our prurient desire, but because the males needed to be kept in their state. First, to be more beautiful and vulnerable with their erections swinging out from their bodies; second, because their erections left them so helpless, more subservient in a way that could never have been achieved otherwise.

The conversation was brilliant. We all discussed the various bodies in front of us. Madame thought Keith the most adorable and commented on his rounded ass and its blond coloring that would be made even more adorable if the crop were used on it. Phil was torn, unable to hide his attraction to Carl, unwilling to deny his excitement at Francois's personal proclivities.

Adrienne was more discreet, asking questions more than making comments. At one point Martin went around the men and removed the clamps and sucked on their tits. Each one of them reacted violently. "Why?"

"The clamps cut off circulation after a certain point," I explained. "To remove them forces a surge of blood into the flesh and a sharp pain. Then, after, they're much more sensitive. But, if he uses his tongue to massage them, they can take more of the agony and he creates more pleasure for them."

Christopher, of course, was the one who reacted most strongly. That, I was sure, was because his audience was so close and so cold as much as anything else. We simply watched the actions that Martin made and the reactions in Christopher that he created.

"That young one," Madame said, referring to Keith, "is certainly darling. But this one has great potential." She took her long painted nails and used them to lightly scratch the underside of Christopher's testicles, lifting his sac up with the ends of her red claws.

"He is one who, shall we say, has many more realistic possibilities for you than any of the others."

"Oh." Her eyebrow arched and her nails suddenly came together in a sharp scissor motion and Christopher's midsection tried desperately to lift itself up off the table and away from her, something that couldn't be done because of Martin's handiwork.

Francois came around with more tea for Adrienne and Phil, more wine for Madame and me. The conversation continued, but moved on to the business of the convention. Phil and Adrienne were the two least acquainted of us and they found many people that they knew in common that they'd never had a chance to discuss before. Contracts were being negotiated on the floor of the association meeting. Editors were changing jobs. Each of us was a devoted fan of the others in the room and had to make appreciative comments on each other's work.

As though the commercial and literary discussions needed to be balanced, Martin went into his next stage. He brought out a handsome new leather strap I'd bought and vaguely wandered through the room. He delivered a substantial, but not violent, blow to the buttocks of each of the men. Keith and Sean followed him as best they could with their eyes, trying to prepare themselves. Francois sped up his service of food and drink, trying to avoid my overseer's lash. Glen and Phillip were wild in their total helplessness against the columns. Carl refused to display the least bit of concern.

This wasn't any kind of performance. Martin could have done that, I certainly knew he could. That was not the purpose here. This was simply part of the atmosphere. We four guests ignored it all, other than to make very occasional glances at his handiwork.

It went on for an hour and a half. Madame and I were — I knew — ecstatic. It was perfect. Adrienne was flushed with excitement and, even if she would never be one of us, the sight of it and the invitation to be present was precisely the gift she'd wanted that I could produce. Phil was simply smiling. I thought he was probably remembering some party in Paris, or Berlin, perhaps London or Rome.

"I must go," he finally said. He stood.

Adrienne rose with him. "I must also. It's been astonishing."

"Would you like Francois's number?" I asked Phil.

"I'd like Francois," he joked back.

"Then, by all means. You shouldn't take public transportation across the Bay alone in any event." I gave Francois some orders, made some quick and simple arrangements for him to return to gather his things, then had him dress.

"You're giving him away?" Adrienne was standing there, her beautiful dress and her lighted cigarette couldn't keep her from giving the impression of being stunned.

"To Phil, for this one night..."

"Marvelous."

I realized then that the single act struck her more than any other.

They left. Madame and I went back to our couch and I poured her more wine. The boys were utterly gorgeous now. The time in their bondage was beginning to tell on them. Their bodies were slick with sweat, their movements were more furious and when Martin went through them this time to remove their clamps and suck their nipples, they were truly in agony.

The room was filled with a masculine odor from it all. Glen was crying now, so, too, was Keith.

"Marvelous." It was Madame who made the announcement this time. "I will go." It was over. This level of intensity couldn't be sustained and to move on to another one seemed to distress her, it would have made this one less perfect, I suspect.

Martin got her coat and saw her to the door. They kissed there, moving slowly back to the stuff of their long friendship.

"Shall I send this Christopher to you?" I called out.

She turned back. "Yes, and quickly." Then she left.

Martin and I went about the business of untying the men. I kept the discipline sharp. Glen and Phillip were ordered to kneel in their place by the pillars. Keith and Sean were unbound, but told not to move. Christopher was sent to the shower.

"You like very dominant women," I told him when he came out. "This is the chance for your ultimate." I held out a piece of paper with Madame's hotel name and address. "Do you want it?"

"I've done so much this weekend..." he said it in such a way I thought he was going to say no. But instead, "It wouldn't seem right to stop now." He rubbed his sore nipples and smiled at me. "What was it the old man said to you, 'You son of a bitch?'"

"Get out before you get the strap."

"Yes, sir." Then, in a move that surprised me, he kissed me.

I poured wine into some glass bowls that Francois had brought with his things, and put them on the floor in the center of the room. I took the strap that Martin had been using and stood there with it. "Come and join the party," I told my naked slaves.

They moved, with various degrees of tentativeness and eagerness, towards the bowls, anxious for the liquid, and suspicious of the strap. I stood there, letting the leather hang from my hand, and saw their buttocks, all of them striped to some extent or another, and simply enjoyed how beautiful men could be.

My party had begun...

The End

Two days later I was ready to leave. I called the front desk and had them send Joseph to my suite to carry down my bags.

I hadn't seen him since before the party. I hadn't really thought about him. But he was certainly enthusiastic enough when he arrived.

"You really leaving so soon?"

"Joseph, it's been a week."

"And we never did anything," he said with a petulant voice.

"That might be just as well."

"Yeah? I think that party of yours must've been pretty kinky, man. We were all talking about it."

"What did you know to talk about?"

"The studs you got coming up here all at once. And those two women. They were something, themselves. What were they doing there?"

"Enjoying themselves, that's all."

"You shouldn't be so selfish. I could've enjoyed myself, too, you know."

"I doubt it, Joseph."

He carried my bags down the hallway to the elevator and through the lobby. He called a cab for me and opened the door. But he wouldn't let me simply enter the taxi.

"You worry about me enjoying your party, huh?" I wasn't at all sure what he meant.

He smiled and reached into his hip pocket. He brought out a

copy of one of Adrienne's most recent — and most intense — sexual fantasy books. Her picture was on the cover. He showed it to me. "You shouldn't underestimate people, man. I think I could have had a good time at your party."

With that, I laughed and got in the cab. It was a long journey home.

THE MASTER'S JOURNALS WILL CONTINUE

Other books of interest from ALYSON PUBLICATIONS

THE ALEX KANE BOOKS:

☐ *#1:* **SWEET DREAMS,** by John Preston, $5.00. In this, the first book of the series, Alex Kane travels to Boston when he hears of a ruthless gang preying on gay teenagers; in so doing he meets his future partner, Danny Fortelli.

☐ *#2:* **GOLDEN YEARS,** by John Preston, $5.00. Operators of a shady nursing home think they can make a profit by exploiting the dreams of older gay men — but they haven't reckoned with the Alex Kane factor.

☐ *#3:* **DEADLY LIES,** by John Preston, $5.00. Kane goes after a politician who's using homophobia to advance his own political career.

☐ *#4:* **STOLEN MOMENTS,** by John Preston, $5.00. Kane takes on a tabloid publisher in Texas, who has decided that he can take advantage of homophobia to increase his paper's circulation.

☐ **HOT LIVING: Erotic stories about safer sex,** edited by John Preston, $8.00. The AIDS crisis has encouraged gay men to look for new and safer forms of sexual activity; here, over a dozen of today's most popular gay writers erotically portray those new possibilities.

☐ **I ONCE HAD A MASTER and other tales of erotic love,** by John Preston, $8.00. One of this country's best-known writers of erotic gay male fiction here tells the story of a man's journey through the S/M world, beginning with another man as his master and ending in that role himself.

☐ **ALL-AMERICAN BOYS,** by Frank Mosca, $5.00. "I've known that I was gay since I was thirteen. Does that surprise you? It didn't me...." So begins *All-American Boys,* the story of a teenage love affair that should have been simple — but wasn't.

☐ **MEDITERRANEO,** by Tony Patrioli, $12.50. Through exquisite photos, Italian photographer Tony Patrioli explores the homoerotic territory in which, since the beginning of time, adolescent boys have discovered sex. (Oversized paperback)

☐ **IN THE TENT,** by David Rees, $6.00. Seventeen-year-old Tim realizes that he is attracted to his classmate Aaron, but, still caught up in the guilt of a Catholic upbringing, he has no idea what to do about it until a camping trip results in unexpected closeness.

☐ **THE HUSTLER,** by John Henry Mackay; trans. by Hubert Kennedy, $8.00. Gunther is fifteen when he arrives alone in the Berlin of the 1920s. There he is soon spotted by Hermann Graff, a sensitive and naive young man who becomes hopelessly enamored with Gunther. But love does not fit neatly into Gunther's new life.... *The Hustler* was first published in 1926. For today's reader, it combines a poignant love story with a colorful portrayal of the gay subculture that thrived in Berlin a half-century ago.

☐ **THE SPARTAN,** by Don Harrison, $6.00. In the days of the first Olympics, gay relationships were a common and valued part of life. *The Spartan* tells the story of a young athlete and his adventures in love and war, providing a vivid picture of classical Greece, the early Olympics, and an important part of our history.

☐ **MURDER IS MURDER IS MURDER,** by Samuel M. Steward, $7.00. Gertrude Stein and Alice B. Toklas go sleuthing through the French countryside, attempting to solve the mysterious disappearance of their neighbor, the father of their handsome gardener. A new and very different treat from the author of the Phil Andros stories.

☐ **$TUD,** by Phil Andros; introduction by John Preston, $7.00. Phil Andros is a hot and horny hustler with a conscience, pursuing every form of sex — including affection — without apology, yet with a sense of humor and a golden rule philosophy. When Sam Steward wrote these stories back in the sixties, they elevated gay fiction to new heights; today they remain as erotic and delightful as ever.

☐ **EIGHT DAYS A WEEK,** by Larry Duplechan, $7.00. Can Johnnie Ray Rousseau, a 22-year-old black singer, find happiness with Keith Keller, a six-foot-two blond bisexual jock who works in a bank? Will Johnnie Ray's manager ever get him on the Merv Griffin show? Who was the lead singer of the Shangri-las? And what about Snookie? Somewhere among the answers to these and other silly questions is a love story as funny, and sexy, and memorable, as any you'll ever read.

☐ **FRANNY: The Queen of Provincetown,** by John Preston, $5.00. Even if you dressed Franny in full leather, he would still look like a queen. It's the way he walks, his little mannerisms, and his utter unwillingness to change them or hide them that give him away. "The best gay male novel of the year," writes *The Front Page,* Raleigh, N.C.

☐ **SECOND CHANCES,** by Florine de Veer, $7.00. Is it always harder to accept what is offered freely? Jeremy could easily have the love of his devoted friend Roy, yet he chooses to pursue the handsome and unpredictable Mark instead.

☐ **THE BUTTERSCOTCH PRINCE,** by Richard Hall, $5.00. When Cordell's best friend and ex-lover is murdered, the only clue is one that the police seem to consider too kinky to follow up on. So Cordell decides to track down the killer himself — with results far different from what he had expected.

☐ **CLASSIFIED AFFAIRS,** by John Preston and Frederick Brandt, $7.00. How do you write a personal ad that really will catch people's attention? What should you expect when you place an ad? When you reply? Here are answers to all those questions, and more — interspersed with numerous actual ads that the authors found memorable, funny or intriguing.

These titles are available at many bookstores, or by mail.

— — — — — — — — — — — — — —

Enclosed is $_____ for the following books. (Add $1.00 postage when ordering just one book; if you order two or more, we'll pay the postage.)

_____ _____

_____ _____

_____ _____

name: _____ address:_____

city: _____ state: _____ zip: _____

ALYSON PUBLICATIONS
Dept. B-94, 40 Plympton St., Boston, Mass. 02118

After June 30, 1988, please write for current catalog.